Blessing on the Run

by Alana Terry

The characters in this book are fictional. Any resemblance to real persons is coincidental. No part of this book may be reproduced in any form (electronic, audio, print, film, etc.) without the author's written consent.

Copyright © July 2017 Alana Terry

CHAPTER 1

You'd think they'd call it morning sickness because it makes you sick in the morning, wouldn't you? Oh, well. Mysteries of life, all that junk.

We're late to my parents', which is no real surprise. I just hate to disappoint them.

Again.

Here's Blessing, twenty minutes late.

I can hear it now.

I turn around in my seat. Make sure Tyson's presentable.

"Baby, don't you know your pants got holes in them?"

He doesn't look up from his iPad.

"And you better not plan to stare at that screen all night. We're going to Grandma and Grandpa's to talk to folks and have a good time. You got that?"

He gives me a grunt in response, which is about all I can expect of him these days. Kid's in preschool and he's already going through mood swings. Damion in the driver's seat's getting ready to make a scene, but I touch his arm and whisper, "It's ok." The last thing Tyson needs is for my boyfriend to blow up all over him. It's Christmas Eve. Time for love and harmony and family together, all that stuff and nonsense, as Dad would say.

Man, I can't believe how bloated I feel. There's no way I can hide the pregnancy from my parents much longer. I just hate to think of the disappointment on their faces.

Again.

You'd think by now pregnancy would be a breeze, wouldn't you? Carrying your boyfriend's child in your thirties when you both have jobs and a home to live in's got to be easier than being a little twelve-year-old ward of the state too scared to tell your foster parents that your uncle got you knocked up, right?

And there've been two other pregnancies between then and now, so it's not like I'm new at this.

But I'm still terrified of telling my parents. Maybe some things never change.

Mom and Dad will have to learn the truth eventually. Damion can't figure out why it's such a big secret, but he doesn't understand my parents. I mean, he's with them enough. They invite us over for Sunday lunch or big holiday meals like this all the time, but that doesn't mean Damion really *knows* them.

Dad's as conservative as they get. Seriously, with that James Earl Jones voice he's got plus how right-winged he is and all into his evangelical Christian preaching, you'd think he'd be hosting one of those conservative AM radio talk shows instead of just listening to them like some sort of news addict.

He's a pastor on top of that, so you can imagine how fun my life was when I moved in with him and Sandy as a preteen who was too scared to mention the fact I was pregnant. Didn't get adopted until a few years later, but that had more to do with the state paperwork than anything else. They've always been Mom and Dad from as long as I can remember, even if I didn't call them that right away.

It's strange that I think about the past so much these days. As if I didn't have problems of my own. And I'm not talking about the fact that my dad's the pastor of one of the largest churches in the Cambridge area and I'm pregnant with my on-again, off-again boyfriend's baby and my folks don't even have a clue. I've been nervous ever since I found out about this baby, but right now I've got bigger things to worry about.

I've got all the regular stress of the holidays and all those obligations to buy gifts with money that doesn't exist, I've got a son who's about to get expelled from preschool if he keeps getting into fights, and I've got a psychotic ex-boyfriend/former pimp making death threats against me and my kid and my extended family.

Merry Christmas, right?

Most wonderful time of the year.

CHAPTER 2

My parents' house is decked out like normal. Tyson's been telling me about all the baking he and Mom have been doing on those days she watches him while I'm at work, but you never fully appreciate just how much that woman cooks until you walk into her dining room and see the spread.

Seriously, I think there are small countries in Africa you could feed with all this surplus.

Mom wraps her arms around me the second I step through the front door, and I feel myself stiffen. That woman's so intuitive I'm almost surprised when she lets me go without asking when the baby's due.

She'll be excited for another grandchild. That's just the way she is. It's Dad I'm concerned about. I know the news is going to take him completely by surprise. In his mind, I'm the same little twelve-year-old girl he and Mom took in so many years ago, this pure little innocent thing.

As if I was pure and innocent at that point, me and my seven-month-old fetus.

Dad shouldn't be surprised I'm knocked up again. Actually, given my history, the really shocking news is that I'm not even more messed up.

Not that my life's been peaches and cream, especially since Jarrod got out of prison.

I didn't even know he was free until he just showed up. I was closing up the bank a couple weeks ago. Hurrying out so I could pick up Tyson from Damion's mom's place and give him an earful for the way he talked back to his teacher earlier that day. I swear, the boy could do fine in preschool except the teacher and workers have it out for him. I defend him to their faces, which is the only reason he hasn't been expelled yet, but when it's just the two of us, you better believe he knows how ticked off I am.

What's with a kid who can't make it through two hours of preschool without getting into a fight with one of his classmates? Seriously? I ask him that all the time. "Honey, why you gotta go making trouble when you know it just makes your teachers mad?"

And he shrugs and says, "I dunno," and makes me wonder if he even realizes that he's doing it. Half the time, I swear he's totally clueless.

He could have started kindergarten last fall, but Mom said he wasn't ready. And I suppose if he's giving his preschool workers that much of a hassle, maybe it's true. But still …

Too smart for his own good. That's what he is. Problem is I don't even remember being that age, so of course I have nothing to compare it to. Far as I know, I was even worse than he is, but there's no way to go back in time and prove that. Only forward.

That's what I keep telling myself.

Keep moving forward.

Which is why it was so hard when Jarrod showed up like a shadow from the past.

He startled me. He's always loved to startle me. Sneak up behind me, grab me by the ribs, and laugh in my face when he made me scream like a little girl.

Which is exactly what I was when we met. So young.

Young and laughing and screaming whenever I got tickled by my step-cousin's teenage uncle.

Well, he did it again just a few weeks ago. Startled me the night I was closing the bank. He's lucky. Some women carry pepper spray or stun guns or things like that. He could have gotten himself hurt.

I turned around, ready to deck whoever attacked me, then I saw him standing there laughing. Head thrown back, just going at it like he was watching the funniest movie in the world.

So I laughed too. Stupid of me. Probably just encouraged him.

Some habits are hard to break.

"What're you doing here?" I asked, and he said, "Oh, just looking for my girl."

I should have called the cops. Called the cops or called my boyfriend. Something. Anything but stand there smiling like an idiot. It's like my body's still reacting to memories that are a decade and a half old by this point.

Memories that make me think we used to have this perfect storybook romance between us.

Man, I hate how stupid I can be.

"How long's it been?" he asked, and like the idiot I am, I knew exactly how much time had passed, right down to the month.

"I didn't think you were getting out until fall," I told him.

And he smiled. Probably happy to discover I'd been keeping track. Eagerly counting down the days.

As if.

"Got off for good behavior. You know how it is."

And I nodded. Yes, I do know how it is, thanks to Jarrod and those things I did for him so many years ago.

"How's your son?" he asked, and that's the first time I remember feeling scared. I'm such a fool. Why didn't I call 911 the minute he showed up? It's not like he was physically preventing me. The desk phone was right there. It would have been easy. If I'd been desperate, I could have even hit that little red panic button behind the counter.

But I stood there trying to change the subject, trying to get him to forget about my boy.

"What you worrying about him for?" I finally asked.

And Jarrod grinned like he had something planned, and I remember feeling nauseated, but it was completely different than morning sickness.

Even then I could have called the police, although my restraining order was several years old. It might have expired, but I wasn't sure. Either way, I should have called them. At the very least demanded to know why they released a felon like him without giving me some kind of warning.

But instead I stood there smiling, hoping to distract him so he'd stop thinking about my boy.

Mom's leading me into the living room, snapping me out of these memories. She's introducing me to some new charity case she's taken into her home. I do my best to act polite, but in the back of my mind, I'm still thinking about Jarrod, the man who called himself my uncle because I was step-related to his niece, the man who stole so much more than my childhood.

Maybe you'd expect me to be dreaming about all the ways I'd kill him if I got the chance or wishing some other slow and painful death on him, which I'm sure he deserves. But no, I'm thinking about that first night he told me he loved me. About the get-rich-quick scheme he came up with, promising me a home in Hawaii, telling me he'd marry me as soon as I hit eighteen.

Then recalling the cold, menacing tone in his voice when he threatened to kill me and everyone I love.

CHAPTER 3

There isn't a college student, exchange student, or single bachelor or bachelorette from my parents' church who wasn't invited here tonight. Whole bunch of strays and loners, plus whatever family managed to make it.

Mom and Dad's house is modest by Medford standards, but they've squeezed thirty or forty or more people here for Mom's famous Christmas Eve dinner.

Mom's been giving me the questioning eye all night. I swear she knows about the baby. Maybe she'll find a way to mention it to Dad, warm him up to the idea of becoming a grandpa again.

No matter how he reacts, it won't be as hard as when I got pregnant with Tyson. Of course, my relationship with my parents at that point in my life was strained at best. I can't say that I'm proud of it, but when you've got a past as convoluted and difficult as mine, you can understand how sometimes people end up with criminal records.

Not that I made all the right decisions. I'm not trying to give you a bunch of excuses, but some folks make things so clear-cut. So black and white. They see a woman arrested for being an accessory to child prostitution and assume she's a felon who deserves to be locked up, kept out of the public eye, prevented from ever having contact with minors and ideally sterilized.

They don't see the x-rays showing the broken ribs or fractured cheekbones. They don't see the photos documenting all the black eyes or finger-sized bruises on your neck. All they see is the label.

It's a small miracle I don't have to register anymore. I know conservatives are the ones who are supposed to be all hard on crime and stuff, but it was my dad who pleaded my case in front of a bunch of lawyers and statesmen. Made me tell my side of the story.

That's when they stopped seeing me as a perpetrator.

That's why I don't have to register anymore.

Thank God.

Jarrod didn't know that. Stupid jerk hadn't even done his homework.

"So your boyfriend know you're a felon?" he asked me that night at the bank. He was standing between me and the exit by then, and he's still more than half a foot taller than I am. Trouble is he also spent nearly all his free time behind bars pumping iron, so he's even stronger now than he was when he got locked up.

Lucky me, right?

I didn't want to talk to him about Damion, but when your ex has just gotten out of prison and shows up at your work when no one else is there and now he's deliberately blocking your chances of escape, you don't have a whole lot of opportunities to call the shots.

I have no idea how he found out about Damion, but that doesn't matter. It's simple for someone like him. Just like discovering where I worked, knowing my schedule so he could be there the one night a week I was on closing.

"What's he look like?" Jarrod asked. "He dark and handsome like me? Big hunk?" He stepped closer, and I remember worrying that I was going to be late picking up my son. Out of all the things I should have been scared of right then, I was worrying that Tyson would have to stay an extra ten or fifteen minutes with Damion's mom.

"He's a good guy," I told Jarrod. "We're just trying to get by. That's all."

"Yeah? What about our house in Hawaii? What about all that money we were gonna make?"

"Hawaii was one big lie, and you know it," I reminded him. "All you needed me for was to keep your other girls in line."

I sounded like a little kid complaining when someone else cuts on the way to the cafeteria.

He reached his hand out and stroked my cheek. I should have pulled away. Even now, I don't know why I didn't.

Old habits.

"Come on, baby. You remember how good we were together, don't you? Tell me something, your man know about us? You tell him about all the good times we had?"

He was talking so sweet I thought maybe he'd let me leave. I tried to squeeze past, but he grabbed me by the shoulder. How could I have forgotten how tight his grip was?

"Where you off to so fast?" His breath was hot in my ear. I can't say it was exactly a tickle, but I remember it sent goosebumps racing up my spine.

"I'm off the clock," I said. "I gotta go."

"Gonna get your son?" he asked.

"That's not your business," I told him. My voice was forceful, but I had stopped trying to strong-arm my way past him.

Sometimes with Jarrod, you learn to just take what's coming and wait for whatever mood he's in to pass.

He ignored my little remark and stood there staring at me. "You look so good," he said, and to this day I thank God that those simple words didn't make me feel anything more than a slight flush. All I wanted to do was go pick up my boy.

He sighed. Cocked his head to the side like I've seen him do thousands of times. "Man, I've missed you."

I could tell that any hint of danger had passed. Funny how after so many years I could still read the signs that well.

"I've gotta go." I brushed by him, and he didn't stop me. "I'll see you around."

"Yeah," he said, so cocky and confident I could see the grin on his face without having to turn to look at him. "See you around."

He spoke the words in a snarl that made my pulse race and my hands start sweating so that by the time I pulled up in front of Damion's mom's house I was still shaking.

CHAPTER 4

"How's my baby?" Dad booms as he wraps me up in a hug. For a split second I'm afraid that Damion's told him about the pregnancy and that's what he's talking about, but then Dad kisses me on the cheek, calls me his little girl, and I understand.

I'm the baby. Just like I always will be in Dad's mind, even though I'm a mother well into my thirties and got pregnant for the first time over two decades ago.

As far as Dad's concerned, I'll always be the scared little girl he met so many years ago.

I'll never forget the day CPS brought me over to my new home. I was all of twelve and a half but was already pregnant with Jarrod's baby. And there were Carl and Sandy looking so tickled to have me join their little picture-perfect family.

Dad and I hit it off right away, which goes completely against everything you'd expect. I mean, if you'd read even the first page or two of my CPS file, you'd understand why I had every reason to mistrust men, especially older authority figures.

Sandy was, well ... you'd have to meet her for yourself. She's like a tsunami of compassion. And for some people, that's exactly what they need, but others like me end up with this feeling like they're going to drown. It wasn't that my foster mother and I didn't get along. Sure, we had our ups and downs, but for the most part we were fine together.

But it was Dad I connected with first. Dad I bonded with the strongest.

Which is why I don't want him to find out about Jarrod.

I saw him twice after that first time at the bank. Looking back, I was stupid not to call the cops right away. And even once I got free from him that night, that should have been the first thing I did, not speeding over to pick up my son and hold him so close.

Couple days passed, and I was foolish enough to hope that I'd seen the last of Jarrod. Should have known better, but some truths are too difficult to accept right away. Your brain needs time to warm up to reality, know what I mean?

He called me a few days later. Don't ask me how he got the number to my cell. When you're someone like Jarrod, you figure out how to do those things. I swear that man has connections all up and down the East Coast, and he uses most of them for things far more villainous than pestering an old girlfriend.

"What you doing?" he asked all gruff, as if I were a little kid supposed to check in with him every night or something.

"That you, Jarrod?" I asked, thankful that Damion was working late. I still hadn't told my boyfriend about running into Jarrod at the bank because I was hoping to act like an ostrich and keep my head buried in the sand. Or maybe that's an emu. I couldn't even tell you the difference. I just know they're both strange as anything I've ever seen.

"Where you at?" He talked like I owed him an explanation for where I'd been and what I'd been doing for the past two days since he'd scared me at the bank.

"What's it to you?"

"Just wondering." His voice got soft again, reminding me of the man I'd fallen in love with over half a lifetime ago.

I was all of ten. How sick is that? Which made him nineteen. And even though things didn't happen between us until another year or two, he started grooming me right from the beginning.

Bringing me little gifts whenever I went to spend the night with my cousin.

Paying her a crisp twenty-dollar bill if she'd help me sneak out of her house so I could go driving with him without anyone knowing. We went to the movies. We went out for ice cream. That man even took me roller-skating. Told everyone we met I was his niece, his beautiful niece, and it was my birthday so he was taking me out for a special treat.

Every day with Jarrod was my birthday.

And the presents ... Everything ranging from pieces of jewelry that he told me cost several hundred dollars to little stuffed Hello Kitty animals because I was so young I still liked junk like that.

By the time I hit sixth grade, things escalated quickly. School was hard for me. Always had been, but junior high was especially brutal. A lot of it had to do with the social cliques. We were really segregated. I'm not talking just race either, although I'm sure that was part of it. And since I've got dark skin most of the white folks thought I was tough or stuck-up, but the black kids weren't all that accepting either, as if my few years bouncing around to different foster families from all kinds of different ethnicities kept me from being "all black."

But even worse than the race issues were just the dumb social circles. Who had the new Adidas shoes and who didn't. Who had a Jansport backpack and who bought generic.

I'd been in the system a couple years by then. This was still a little before I moved in with Carl and Sandy, who eventually adopted me, but none of my other foster families cared about the difference between a fifteen-dollar pair of shoes and a seventy-dollar pair of shoes, so you can guess what I showed up to school wearing. Same thing with winter coats, brand name jeans, you name it.

I still remember how badly I wanted a Calvin Klein T-shirt. I mean, you'd think something like that was so minor, especially since it was literally just a T-shirt, not even one of those cute little cropped tees or junk like that.

But there was something in me that wanted to be all preppy, to fit in with the cool crowd, and those kids all had Calvin Klein shirts, which as I recall were the only kinds of T-shirts that could be worn tucked into your jeans without you looking like a nerd or cowboy wannabe.

When I mentioned it to Jarrod in passing, he took me to the mall that same night (my foster family at the time thought I was staying over with my step-cousin), and he bought me my Calvin Klein shirt and then dropped three hundred dollars on me at Wet Seal. I don't know if you're familiar with that store, but it's where anybody with any sort of social ambition at my junior high shopped.

He picked the clothes and had me try them on and show him. I still have no idea why the worker there didn't find it odd for a twenty-year-old man to be dressing up a preteen in miniskirts and crop tops. Maybe she did think it was strange but was more interested in her fifteen percent commission than any sense of social responsibility.

Or who knows, maybe she actually bought into his line about being my uncle taking me shopping for my birthday.

Things changed for me immediately with my new wardrobe. And then Jarrod started picking me up in his car after school. He had this classic T-Bird, bright shiny blue, and he'd pull up with the windows down and the stereo blaring and then wait for me to come down the front steps with my friends. Sometimes when I got close enough, he'd wink and snap his fingers and say, "Wassup?"

I turned into a little puddle of giggling hormones, and so did my girlfriends, who all envied me.

Can you imagine how cool you feel when you start the year as the nobody at your school and then have someone like Jarrod show up every afternoon to drive you home?

We spent even more time together that summer because my foster parents at the time both worked and we lived close enough to Jarrod's niece they let me ride my bike there. I seriously could go weeks without actually seeing my step-cousin, but I was with Jarrod every single afternoon. I'll just leave it up to your imagination to guess what happened next. By the time I moved in with Carl and Sandy I was more than halfway through a pregnancy that I ended up keeping secret from everybody.

And still have. Literally. Jarrod himself doesn't even know the full truth.

You'd think I'd look back and despise myself for falling so hard for him. But there's part of me — I hate to even admit it, that's how dumb it sounds — that wishes we could go back to those days.

Jarrod. Me. Sneaking around because we were completely in love (or at least I know I was and he told me he was, so what reason did I have to doubt?).

The stupid thing is that even knowing what I know now, even with all the warning signs, the restraining orders, the run-ins with the law, everything, if I were that little girl again today, I know I'd fall for him just as hard, make all the same mistakes I did back then.

Which is why I'm so scared now that he's out of prison and is trying to maneuver his way back into my life.

"Have some more of the ham, sweetie pie," Mom tells me. I'm busy trying to keep track of my son, who's already spilled punch on some pinch-faced lady's lap, stained Mom's tablecloth trying to double-dip the chips into the nacho cheese, and has probably filled himself with a thousand calories or more of brownies and cookies before he even thought of touching his dinner.

Meanwhile, Dad and Damion have been deep in discussion, which I hope is good news. Dad's never thought too highly of my boyfriend, even though Damion's been working steady at the pizza place for nearly a year now and has never once treated me wrong.

He's not a thing like Jarrod.

I forget if it was when I was in eighth or ninth grade when I first saw Jarrod's anger issues. It wasn't directed at me, or I might have been smart enough to run away. No, who am I kidding? He had me at "Wassup?" How pathetic is that?

Anyway, it was his niece, my step-cousin, who got on the wrong end of his temper. I honestly don't remember what the big deal was. Isn't that funny, especially considering how I literally rolled myself into the corner and sobbed while he hit her.

It wasn't the most injury I'd see him inflict. In the years to come, I'd witness far worse and eventually become the favored victim, but it shook me up that first night.

And what did he do when he finished with my cousin and saw me crying in that scared little ball of nerves and trauma? What'd he do to the little foster girl he'd frightened so badly? Held me against his chest, wiped my tears dry, and promised he'd never yell at me like that.

As long as I never, ever thought of leaving him.

That was our bargain, and I kept up my side of it for decades longer than I should have.

CHAPTER 5

Mom and Dad freaked out when they found me and Jarrod together. I was probably thirteen at the time, and they completely lost it. The way they went at it, you would have thought I was in bed with a terrorist or something. Which honestly isn't that far from the truth, I suppose. Called the cops and everything, but by that point I'd been in love with him for over three years, and I wasn't going to betray him. I gave the police woman a fake name, fake job, fake address, the works.

Anything to protect my truest love.

I made Jarrod my first hundred bucks the summer before I started high school. He was stressed, said that unless he could find a better job he'd have to move back down to Baltimore to live with his buddy and too bad I was too young to offer any real help.

The way he maneuvered the conversation, I came away thinking I dreamed up the idea all on my own. Of course, I was probably the tenth or twentieth or thirtieth girl Jarrod had conned the same way. He knew exactly what he was doing.

"I could try to get some work," I told him, and he sighed.

"The only thing I can think someone like you could do is …" And then he explained.

I didn't want to. Who jumps into that kind of lifestyle *wanting* to? But Jarrod promised me it would only be this one time, and that if I didn't do it he'd have to head to Baltimore and I'd probably never see him again.

What choice did I have?

Obviously, there are people who will look down their noses at me and tell me I had every choice in the world. There's even Bible verses to back them up. Don't ask me the reference. I believe in the Bible and all, I just don't have the chapters memorized, but there's one passage that goes something like "God won't let you be tempted unless he gives you a way out so you don't have to go through with it."

I didn't *have* to go through with it when you look at it that way, but even the law recognizes that there's an age at which a girl really can't be expected to make those kind of choices herself. Can't be held accountable. That's why it's called statutory rape and not statutory sleaziness or something like that.

Maybe you'll think I'm messed up for saying this, but it honestly wasn't that bad. I mean, look at my history, remember? It was hardly different from what my foster brother or my grandpa or my mom's old boyfriend had put me through by then, only this time it was on my terms and I was actually making some money doing it. Money that would keep my true love by my side.

Not the most pleasant of things to be thinking about on Christmas Eve, is it? Mom's at my elbow again, wondering why I'm not eating more. I swear, unless I binge and take in two thousand calories per meal, that woman's convinced I'm anorexic. I allow her to douse my plate with more mashed potatoes and ham but hold off on the gravy. I can't handle grease. I'm past my first trimester but still suffer indigestion that keeps me up for hours.

Not like I don't have other reasons to stay awake worrying.

Like the fact that my ex-boyfriend wants me to help him embezzle funds from the bank where I work.

I knew there had to be an angle from the first time Jarrod showed up and surprised me while I was trying to close, but the real reason didn't come out until he called me about a week later.

It started with the usual types of complaints. "Money's real tight. Nobody wants to hire me when they see my record."

Hmm. Maybe he should have thought of that before he started pimping me and dozens of other underage girls out on the streets, right?

And he expects me to feel sorry for him?

Problem was I did. At least a little. I hate myself for it, but every time I hear his voice, I'm that little girl again who feels such an exhilarating thrill to have the college-aged man offer her a ride home in his T-Bird. And the fact that his hands roam and pinch and bruise the entire trip just means that he thinks I'm pretty, that there's something sexy about me.

As if a junior higher should spend her prepubescence worrying about whether she is or isn't sexy.

At first, I thought he wanted me to go work for him again, and thankfully I had the mental clarity to tell him exactly what I thought about that plan. I'm never going back to the streets. Period.

"Come on," I told him, "you know I'm too old for that now," and then I thought maybe he was going to suggest I do some sort of madam work for him, but I've been his madam before, and as much as my sick and twisted little psyche thought it loved him at one point, I'm not going back to that again either. Not when I have a son and a boyfriend and a respectable job at a bank going for me.

He laughed, told me he was out of that profession (as if I'd ever believe him), and said that what he really wanted was for me to use my bank access to help him and his buddy. Supposedly they had it all planned out. I guess all those years in prison gave him the time and opportunity to expand his network. He didn't fill me in on all the details, just explained what they'd need from me, including the schedule of the bank security workers (which would be easy for me to get a hold of) and one night where I accidentally "forgot" to set the codes when I closed (which could land me in jail).

Problem is Jarrod's not the kind of guy you just tell, "Sorry, not gonna do it, why don't you get lost?" So I made excuses about how I was already on probation at my job (which I wasn't, and he saw through that lie right away) and how I was trying to straighten up my life (which has been the gospel truth for at least the past five years).

Don't ask me why I thought someone like Jarrod would care about me straightening out. He didn't, and it only took one more surprise visit, this time right after I dropped Tyson off at my mom's, for his polite suggestions to turn into threats.

"You don't get me that security schedule, I'll burn your parents' house down." The problem was I knew he was capable of that, and I also knew he was smart enough to set it up so he'd never get caught. There's no way Jarrod would be careless enough to let them connect it back to him. And since he was the reason I had to register as a sex offender for three years of my adult life (as if I had any choice in the ages of the girls my live-in boyfriend was pimping out), my witness would be stained if I tried to testify against him. Any jury would come away thinking I was just some jilted girlfriend out for revenge.

And then came the real kicker. Remember how I said Jarrod's the only one who knows about that first pregnancy? The one way back when I was twelve years old and just moved in with Carl and Sandy?

My hormones were still a kid's at that stage in my life, and by the time Jarrod figured out what was going on (he realized it before I did), there was no doctor in the entire East Coast who'd perform an abortion. At least that's what he told me, but I'm sure it also had to do with the fact that a grown man Jarrod's age couldn't walk a little girl like me into an abortion clinic without raising all kinds of red flags.

So he came up with a plan of his own to take care of our "problem," and when I refused to be part of his bank scheme last week, he threatened to tell the authorities what I'd done. I figured he was bluffing. He couldn't really do that without incriminating himself too, and I told him so, but he came back with a whole bunch of legal jargon about statutes of limitations, things I'd never understand without a law degree. But he made it out like he'd find a way so I'd be the only one to get in trouble.

I'm not about to let him expose me to the world, so I bought myself some time. Told him the security schedule was constantly changing because of the holidays, but after Christmas I could get it for him.

Which is why (in addition to the pregnancy hormones) I can't eat a single morsel Mom prepared for tonight's big feast without it sitting and festering in my gut like moldy cheese or rotten produce.

The thing is, Jarrod still thinks I'm going to work with him.

He still expects me to help him rob that bank, and if I don't, he's going to let everyone know what I did to that little baby so many years ago.

CHAPTER 6

Dad's standing up now, offering the Christmas Eve toast. Does it every year, and every year we tip back our goblets, shout "Cheers," and down our sparkling apple cider in unison. It's been this way since my very first Christmas at Mom and Dad's.

Some things never change.

Like the fact that Jarrod assumes I'll bend over and do whatever he tells me to do.

Even risk unemployment or prison time by helping him rob a bank.

How much have I already agreed to?

It's stupid of me. I don't mean to go through with any of it. I actually like my job. Sure, some of my co-workers are royal pains, but the bank's been good for me. It's kept me clean and dry for longer than any other place I've been. True story.

I told him I'd help because I needed extra time. Time to figure out how seriously to take his threats.

I don't need his drama over the holidays. Tomorrow's Christmas, we're all going to enjoy ourselves for the day, and after that I'll decide what to do. I still don't know if it's something I should talk to my bank supervisor about or the head of security or if it would be better to go straight to the police. Dad would know how to handle it, but he hates Jarrod, and I don't want to ruin his Christmas. He doesn't even know he's out of prison.

Not to mention everything about the baby.

No matter what happens, I've got to keep that part from my parents. They've spent enough decades worrying over me. Grieving over my poor choices.

Dad's busy thanking God for his blessings, and I wonder if Jarrod would really find a way to hurt my parents if I don't help him at the bank.

Does he know I'm planning to back out?

Or is that even the plan anymore?

Sometimes I wonder if I'm really going to talk to security or get the police involved. Maybe I'm not. Maybe I'm still the same girl who let Jarrod sell her to strangers, the same kind of girl who trained workers for him when they're still years too young to get a learner's permit.

The kind of girl who would do just about anything to keep her secret hidden.

Maybe I'm not going to turn him into the police at all.

Maybe I'm just telling myself what I want to hear so I can go to bed with a clean conscience.

Not that I sleep at all anyway. Some of that can be blamed on the baby though. Not quite five months yet, and she's already kicking. At least the doctors say it's a girl, but I have my doubts.

After all I've gone through, after all my failures, God would never trust me with another daughter.

I raise my glass along with everyone else, even though I haven't been listening very carefully to Dad's toast. And then, before I know what's happening, my boyfriend is standing up and looking like a complete idiot.

"I have something to say, too." I try to get him to sit down. He has no idea what he's doing.

"Come on," he whispers to me. "Get up." But I refuse. There is no way I'm joining him while he makes a fool of himself in front of my son, my parents, and several dozen dinner guests.

When Damion finally realizes I'm dead serious, he leaves me alone in my chair and clears his throat. "Well, with this being Christmas and all, and Christmas being a time for, you know, *family,* and all …"

Oh, no he isn't. I do my best to kill him by sheer willpower, but it doesn't work.

He shuffles from one foot to the other like he's got a bad case of jock itch and stammers, "And with Christmas being about the *birth* of baby Jesus, and his mama being pregnant for the holidays and everything ..."

Oh, yes he is. I try one more time to pull him down to his chair. He has no idea what kind of chaos he's about to unleash.

Apparently, Dad's growing impatient with this whole nervous exchange because he shouts, "Spit it out, man!" and Damion says loud enough for everyone in the whole blasted house to hear, "We're gonna have a baby."

I swear, if I didn't hate the thought of starting the dating game all over, if I didn't love Damion in spite of how mad he's making me right now, I'd kill him.

I'd honestly stand up and kill him.

It's not like we're the most likely of couples. Even the way we met is far from romantic. It was at a red light. True story. He rear-ended me, nothing too serious, but we both got out of the car to exchange insurance information. I was fuming mad because he was going to make me late for work on my second day after a big promotion. I was in such a rush I couldn't even remember what he'd looked like when he called me up that weekend to see if I wanted to catch a movie.

Real steamy stuff, right?

But we've been good for each other. In some ways. I've lost track of how many times we've broken up in the past three years and then gotten back together, but it's enough that I didn't even cry the last time it happened, and sure enough it was less than a week before we had hooked up again.

Damion's good for me. Stable. I used to go for the real bad boy type, which I suppose is obvious given what you know about me and Jarrod. Damion's not like that. Sure, he's got enough tats on his arms and back and shoulders that I suppose he might look intimidating to some, but he's got the temperament of a butterfly.

True story.

Which is partly why I love him and partly why he drives me completely insane.

In Damion's mind, if two people fall in love and get pregnant and want to have a baby together, that's great news. He doesn't stop to think about things like church gossips or the Ten Commandments or conservative parents who probably don't appreciate this surprise announcement of their illegitimate grandchild.

Well, there's Damion for you. He can't take it back, but I'm definitely planning to let him know what I think on our way home, which now might happen quite a bit earlier than he first expected.

I'm so busy figuring out everything I'm planning to say to him that I don't even realize he's still standing.

"What are you doing?" I hiss, and he answers, "Just trust me."

As if.

Except now he's not looking at me. He's looking at my dad.

Could his timing be any worse?

Damion's talking to my dad and stuttering. "I, uh, wanted to tell you that I know your daughter's really special to you, and she's really special to me, too, and I know that you being a pastor and all probably doesn't mean you want to have … What I'm trying to say, sir, is I really want to do right by your daughter, by Blessing here."

"I know her name," Dad responds in a complete monotone.

Great.

"And, so, to get to the point, sir …"

"I wish you would," Dad huffs.

Damion wipes his face on a napkin and I swear he could wring out all the extra sweat into a cup. "So, what I really want is I want to ask Blessing to marry me."

Oh, no he didn't.

Mom's face has melted into a puddle of smiles and excitement, and I swear she's about to start blubbering. Meanwhile, I'm trying to control my rage so I don't literally kill this man who just humiliated me in front of all my parents' friends and then had the nerve to propose.

"I know it's maybe not the best time, but I thought, you know, Christmas being all about family and stuff ..."

"Yes." What was that? My dad's talking so quietly I can hardly hear.

Damion's eyes are as wide as the handprint Christmas ornaments I made that are still hanging on the tree. "You're saying it's ok?"

Dad shrugs. "It's fine by me, man, but I'm not the one you need to ask."

Damion nearly trips as he drops to his knee in front of me. He's holding out a small jewelry box to the sound of multiple *ooo*s and *aww*s around the room.

Oh, yes he did.

"Blessing Lindgren, will you marry me?"

I think back over our three-year relationship. Like the first date where he couldn't even get the movie time right and we ended up walking around for two hours in the rain since we already missed the show.

The first breakup and how devastating it was because it made me realize how many things about him I'd come to take for granted.

The joy of getting back together, like we were given the chance to fall in love for a second time.

And a third.

And then a fourth.

How with Jarrod and his threats, with how unsafe I feel, I could use stability in my life.

The kind of stability I've always found when I'm with Damion.

"Yes." I smile in spite of my resolve to stay mad at him. He slips the ring on my finger, saying something corny about me making him the happiest man in the world. While everyone claps and gushes, including my mom only two seats down, he kisses me on the lips, and just like that I'm engaged.

CHAPTER 7

"Geeze, the way you're acting you'd think I just burned down your parents' house instead of proposing to you."

Damion's reference to my mom and dad's home hits too close. Of course, he's right. From the moment we got into the car to drive back to our place, I've been letting him hear how I feel, but obviously he doesn't know about Jarrod or the way he threatened to hurt my family if I didn't do exactly what he demanded.

But I'm way too stressed for this kind of argument. It's Christmas Eve. I don't have time or energy for this. I haven't wrapped any of the presents (not that there will be many), and Mom's expecting us back at her place to watch Tyson open his stocking by nine tomorrow morning. With as poorly as I'm sleeping on top of all the stress about Jarrod — stress that my now-fiancé has no idea about because I haven't mentioned a word about it — I really can't handle an argument.

Which doesn't exactly explain why I'm yelling, but there's irony for you, right?

"Next time, you talk to me before blurting out our business in front of everyone like that."

"Calm down," he tells me, like I'm some child who needs to be soothed. "Everyone was happy for us. Even your dad."

"I don't care what everyone was for us. What I care about is that you completely ignored all that we'd talked about when it came to us, the pregnancy, everything. Because you had to do it your way, just like always. Do house hunting your way so I'm raising my son in a freaking ghetto. Do our engagement your way so I'm totally humiliated on Christmas Eve. Do birth control your way, and now

I'm fat and nauseous and can't keep anything down …"

His knuckles are strained on the steering wheel, but I don't care. If he didn't want a scene, he shouldn't have made one at my parents'. And on Christmas Eve. Thank God Tyson's spending the night over there and doesn't have to see us fight like this. That boy loves Damion so much he'd probably take his side, anyway.

My cell rings. It's Jarrod. I can't even. Why does he keep bothering me? Didn't I tell him to wait until after the holidays?

"Hello." I'm so angry I don't even care that I'm talking to an ex-boyfriend my now-fiancé knows nothing about. An ex-boyfriend with secrets devastating enough that Damion would never forgive me if he found out.

"What do you want?" I demand.

"Woah," Jarrod says, his voice full of fake hurt. "Merry Christmas to you too, babe."

"Why are you calling?"

Damion glances over at me, but I shoot him such an angry stare he won't dare look at me again for the rest of this conversation.

"Calm down. It's the holidays, remember?"

I can't stand the way his voice is so soothing, the way I remember falling to sleep listening to him talking on the phone with his business partners. A voice that could lull me into oblivion no matter how stressed out or anxious I was feeling.

A voice that reminds me of happier days.

No, that's the nostalgia talking. Nothing else. Jarrod is part of my past, and I need to keep him there where he belongs. I'm an engaged woman now. An engaged pregnant woman with a five-year-old son I'm trying my hardest to keep from getting kicked out of yet another preschool. I don't have energy for this low-life convict. I've already wasted enough years on him.

"What do you want?"

He still has that casual, cool sound to his voice. He's probably not only drunk but totally stoned. Stupid. I should have called the cops on him the very first night he came into the bank. "I just want to talk to you. I miss you."

The sad thing is if I weren't so mad at Damion for embarrassing me like that at my parents', I might allow myself the luxury of enjoying that familiar tone, the soothing rhythm. God knows how many nights we spent together completely strung out, perfectly content in our own little world.

The rest of life with him may have been hell, but those nights together were paradise.

I have to stop. Have to snap myself out of this hypnosis. I remember how mad I am at my fiancé and redirect that anger toward Jarrod. "If you don't have anything important to tell me, just leave me alone."

"All right. If that's how you feel." He doesn't sound hurt, which I hate to admit is disappointing. Does he care that I'm pushing him away?

Of course he doesn't.

"Just wanted to know if you've thought any more about my little proposition," Jarrod says.

I am so ready for this man to be out of my life. "No."

"No, you haven't thought about it?"

"No, I'm not going to do it," I correct him. "Not only that, but I'm calling the cops and letting them know you've broken your restraining order."

"That piece of paper is so old it's not even worth the ink it's printed with," he tells me.

Damion is looking at me cautiously now, but I ignore him. Whatever questions he's got will have to wait.

"Just leave me alone and stop trying to call." I hope my voice comes across as stubborn and angry as I feel. I've been accused of giving Jarrod mixed messages in the past, a mistake I certainly can't afford to repeat right now. "I don't want to hear from you again."

"What about our deal, babe? We were gonna cut you in twenty percent for your help."

"I don't care about your deal, and if I hear one more word from you about it, I'm telling security. You hear me?"

"Yeah, I hear you." His voice turned expressionless and cold, like ice pricks in my spine. "You sure you don't want to reconsider?"

I sense the warning in his tone and recall those threats he's made in the past, but right now I'm too pumped full of adrenaline and rage to care. I've got the law on my side, I'm not taking any risks now that things are finally starting to shape up in my life, and if he's going to rob a bank, it's not going to be on my watch.

"No, I'm not going to reconsider." This time, there's no question whether or not I'm sending mixed signals. Anyone within a mile could hear me loud and clear. True story.

"I'm sorry to hear that." He lowers his voice and adds, "But not nearly as sorry as you're gonna be."

CHAPTER 8

Damion's staring at me like I just told him I'm pregnant with a water buffalo. As soon as I got off the phone, he wanted to know what that conversation was about, and it's taken me all the way until now to fill him in on just the minor details.

He sits with a half-eaten plate of nachos in front of him in our cluttered living room. I told myself I'd clean up before Christmas, but the stress from having Jarrod jump back into my life coupled with how tired I've been from this pregnancy kept me from my good intentions.

I hate living like this, but I suppose it's more than I deserve. At least we're out of government housing, and even though we can barely afford rent we still haven't fallen behind. Thank God people tend to tip Damion more around the holidays or we couldn't afford our heating bill in this drafty apartment.

"So are you going to call the cops?" he asks once I tell him the entire story. Everything except for Jarrod's threat to expose my secret about the baby.

I shrug. "Not unless he keeps bothering me. But I think he's gone for good." I hope my voice sounds more certain than I feel.

"I can't believe you didn't tell me this sooner." He's abandoned his plate of nachos and is now pacing the length of the living room. All ten feet of it.

"Calm down," I say. "I didn't tell you because it was something I knew I could handle on my own. Which I just did."

Damion mumbled something under his breath.

Seriously? We're going to get into *another* fight?

"What'd you say?"

Damion stops pacing. "I said maybe that's our problem right there."

It's a good thing Damion's never dreamed of becoming a comedian because of that terrible timing.

"You're going to start this right now? On Christmas Eve?" I add in case he's forgotten what day it is.

"I'm not the one starting it. You started it in the car when you ripped into me for *proposing to you.*"

"I never asked you to propose to me!" It's a dumb thing to say, but it's the first thing that jumps into my head.

"Of course not. That's why it's called a *proposal.*"

"What's that supposed to mean?" I demand, and apparently he doesn't know because he grabs his plate of nachos and slams it onto the counter for no reason.

"Most girls are happy to get engaged."

"You know that from firsthand experience?" I ask. "You done this sort of thing before?"

There's no reason for me to egg him on, but I don't care. He's the one who started it.

He stands in front of me, his hands balled into fists, but I'm not worried. I've survived Jarrod. Does Damion think I'd be scared of him?

"I can't believe how selfish you're acting," he says.

So now I'm selfish because I'm not gushing over the ring he forced on me with everyone watching? A ring I never asked for and certainly didn't want this Christmas?

I pry it off my fingers. He didn't even bother to find out my size, and with my hands all swollen from the pregnancy it's nearly impossible to wrench loose.

"What are you doing?" he demands.

"Giving this back." I finally wrench it free and shove it into his palm. "Maybe next time you'll actually listen when a girl tells you she's not ready to talk to her family."

He's staring at me like I just sprouted demon horns. I get up and head toward the door.

"Wait," he says. "Where are you going?"

"To my parents'. And don't bother stopping by tomorrow either. I'll text you to figure out a time I can come and get my things."

"You're leaving?"

Give the boy a genius point. "Get out of my way," I huff. I don't even bother with a coat as I yank the keys off their holder, fling open the front door, and storm out into the dark, wintery night.

CHAPTER 9

"Maybe you both need a little time to cool down," Mom's telling me over tea and cookies in her dining room. I feel bad keeping her up so late. It's past eleven, and I know she's not going to even think of getting to bed before she's cleaned up after her thirty or forty dinner guests. I should be helping her with the dishes, not sucking her time and energy by making her sit and listen to my problems, but each time I offer to lend a hand she tells me she'll take care of it all in the morning.

As if.

"Of course, you're welcome to stay here as long as you need," she assures me. "Your father and I would actually feel better if the two of you weren't living together before the wedding. It's something we've always ..."

"There's not going to be a wedding." I sound like Tyson when he's throwing a temper tantrum, but I don't care. Mom's walked with me and prayed with me through an abusive boyfriend, all those legal proceedings, and countless drug detoxes. I think she's strong enough to handle my pity party.

She reaches over and pats my hand, making little *tut tut* noises with her tongue. For a moment, I want nothing more than to bury my head against her chest and let her stroke my hair like she did when I was little.

Instead, I let out a massive sigh.

"Christmas is always a hectic time," she says. "Give it a few days before you make any major decisions."

Sometimes Mom surprises me. Here she is, the wife of the East Coast's most conservative, old-fashioned pastor. Her pregnant daughter's just broken up with her live-in-boyfriend-turned-fiancé, and instead of preaching against the shame and sinfulness of cohabitation or blaming all our relationship problems on the fact that we hopped into bed together before exchanging vows, she's actually encouraging me to not give up on him.

True story.

We talk a little longer. I still haven't mentioned Jarrod, his threats, or the way he tried to coerce me into helping him steal funds from my employer. I certainly haven't mentioned the baby she doesn't even know I conceived so many years ago. Mom's got enough on her plate.

Part of me thinks I should call the police, but I worry about the tables being turned and me becoming the perpetrator instead of the victim. There are men on the police force — I'm absolutely convinced of it — who think that I should still be listed as a registered sex offender, who think that just because Jarrod was pimping out underaged girls and I knew about it when we were together that I was somehow voluntarily perpetuating my boyfriend's crimes.

It doesn't matter to them that he'd threaten my family any time I even thought of leaving. Doesn't make any difference that on the night of his arrest, I was cooperative. I'm even the one who *let* the policemen into the house to rescue all the girls Jarrod had kept imprisoned there.

I let them in because I thought they were there to rescue me, too.

Unfortunately, since I'd been with Jarrod the longest by then, since I was technically an adult at the time, and since I was the one who did the younger girls' makeup because otherwise my boyfriend would have beat them and me both until we passed out, I was complicit in his crimes.

As if.

So that's why I'm not too keen on calling the cops. That, of course, and the whole thing about the baby.

I'm not even ready to think about that yet.

"Well ..." I stand up. Mom does too and wraps her arms around my neck. She smells like lavender shampoo and those static-free laundry sheets she tosses in the dryer.

"You ready for bed?" she asks. "We can move Tyson upstairs to the ..."

"Don't worry about it." I've already decided to share a bed with my son tonight. He can be a little terror at school and at home, but when he's asleep he's a perfect angel. "I'll just cuddle up with Tyson," I tell Mom, and she gives me a smile. I don't know what it means, but I sense the maternal love behind it.

Our good-night ritual involves several more hugs plus Mom praying for me like I'm still a little twelve-year-old girl afraid to go to sleep in a brand-new foster home. Finally, I make my way down the hall to where Tyson's snoring lightly in the twin bed pushed up beneath the window.

BLESSING ON THE RUN

I curl up behind him. He's gotten so big. It literally hurts to think about him growing up. What if he ends up like Jarrod?

I shove my ex out of my thoughts as if he were a spider or beetle invading a summer picnic, nestle up against my son, and pray for sleep to finally overtake my frazzled nerves.

God knows how bad I need some rest.

CHAPTER 10

I wake up to the sound of pots clanging in the kitchen.

"I'm sorry, dear," Mom says. "I was trying to let you sleep. I know it's been a hard night for you."

I glance around, wondering what I'm doing curled up under piles of quilts on the couch.

"Was Tyson snoring too loud?" she asks.

That's what it was. "Yeah. I hope you don't mind me coming out here."

"Of course not, love. You're welcome anywhere just like this was your own home." Mom winces when she says the words, and I wonder if she's thinking about the apartment and ex-fiancé I left behind last night.

"Is Tyson up yet?" I ask, wondering if he'll be disappointed if my boyfriend misses out on our Christmas traditions. Part of me hopes Damion will be stubborn enough to show up here anyway, but I'm certainly not going to call or text and beg him to come.

I wasn't the one acting like a baby last night.

"He's still asleep," Mom tells me, glancing down the hall toward the back room where I tried to snuggle up last night with my son. "It's only quarter to eight."

Man, I need more sleep. "Got any coffee?" I ask.

Mom pours a mug and dumps in three spoonfuls of sugar and about a quarter cup of half and half. If she's trying to give me diabetes and heart disease before I hit forty, she's going at it the right way.

"Oh, I should have asked if you wanted eggnog instead of creamer." Mom frowns at the mug in her hand. "Want me to dump this out and start over?"

"Eggnog in coffee?" I don't even like the stuff plain. I certainly wouldn't mix it in with anything else, especially not something as important as my first caffeine injection of the day.

I reach out for the mug she's holding. "This will be fine."

Five minutes later, I feel almost human. Almost ready to be happy and joyful this Christmas morning if only for Tyson's sake and nothing else.

But there's more to it than that. This is my chance to prove — to myself, to my son, and to my mom and dad — that I can be happy without Damion. I'm starting to wonder if he was just holding me back.

I realize for the first time I haven't thought about Jarrod or his threats since some point last night when I finally came out of the bedroom to toss and turn on the couch. Then when I woke up, I spent a full ten or twelve waking minutes not remembering him at all.

Probably some kind of record. A Christmas miracle.

I hear the toilet flush and feel inexplicably giddy like I'm still a little girl listening to the sounds of her father waking up on Christmas morning.

I'm hugging Dad before he even steps into the living room. "Merry Christmas." I kiss his cheek, which is slightly stubbly this early in the day before he's shaved. Without his glasses, he looks older for some reason. The slight gray around his temples appears more pronounced.

I kiss him one more time. "How you doing?"

"Good," he answers and glances around the room. "Where's Tyson?"

"Still in bed," I tell him. "You can go wake him up. He had a lot of cookies last night. I'm surprised you guys managed to get him to sleep when you did."

"It was no problem," Mom says as Dad walks down the hall in a tired stupor. He opens the door to my son's room and Mom continues, "Soon as the last guests left, he just crashed. Went to his room and we didn't hear a peep from him since."

"Tyson? Where you at, boy?" Dad calls, and Mom and I both glance up at each other.

I walk down the hall. I don't run. I walk.

"Tyson!" Dad shouts again, and my chest feels like someone's reached in and started squeezing off the blood to my heart.

Dad's out of the room and opening the other doors down the hall. "Did he go upstairs?"

Mom's face is pale, which is saying a lot given how light she is to start with. "I'll go check." Her voice cracks just once.

"Tyson?" I call. "Come on, bud." I make myself sound cheerful so he'll want to come out of whatever hiding place he's found. "It's Christmas morning. Don't you wanna see what Santa put in your stocking?" I don't care that my dad hates the commercialized Santa Claus of childhood fantasy and refuses to entertain such anti-Christian traditions in his home.

I don't even care that my voice is now full of unmasked panic. "Tyson?"

A minute later, Mom comes down the stairs shaking her head. She's trying to look calm, but she has never once been able to tell a lie for as long as I've known her. "Think he's hiding?" she asks, but the fear that's settled in the base of my gut is mirrored in her face.

Dad opens the front door. Calls for my son. We all go to the garage, look in all the corners and even in the car. Mom slips on her boots and fuzzy pink bathrobe and checks the backyard.

We call him dozens of times. Hundreds of times, but there's no answer.

My son has disappeared.

CHAPTER 11

Mom sets plates of food on the table in front of the police officer and me, but I have no appetite. Detective Drisklay drinks black coffee from one of Mom's cute handmade snowman mugs. I think it's the one I colored my first Christmas living with my parents, although I couldn't guarantee it.

"Is there anyone your son plays with in the area? Friends in the neighborhood?" the detective asks.

I glance at Mom, who would know better than I would since she babysits him when he's not at preschool or with Damion's mom.

"No, sir. There's not too many young families in the *cul de sac* anymore, I'm afraid to say. The Richardsons, they had four children, bright kids, very polite too, but their dad got a new job that was closer to his folks, if I remember right."

"Any other ideas where he might be?" Drisklay takes a noisy sip of coffee.

"Let's see." Mom runs her hands over her braided hair. "I think he was going to Michigan. Or was it Montana?"

Detective Drisklay and I stare at Mom like she's just suggested my son is on a journey to the center of the solar system until Dad exclaims, "Not the Richardsons, woman. He's asking about Tyson."

Mom glances at the detective and apologizes sheepishly.

I roll my eyes and finally decide to stop letting some stranger run this meeting. "Listen, I know my son. There's nowhere he would have wanted to be on Christmas morning besides here, unless …"

I stop myself. Try to remember all that Mom and I talked about last night after I stormed away from Damion. I thought Tyson was asleep. Could he have been listening in on our conversation? Still, even if he knew Damion wouldn't be joining us for Christmas, even if he wanted to be with Damion instead of us ...

"My boyfriend and I got into a fight last night," I tell the detective. I'm sure he's used to hearing secrets far darker and dirtier than this, but I still hate to talk to him about something that probably isn't any of his business.

"You did?" Dad interrupts. "What about? Did he hurt you?"

"I'm fine," I insist and focus my attention back on Drisklay. "But I left home and spent the night here and told him not to bother to come over this morning for Christmas."

In my mind, I'm processing everything I've ever known about Damion. He's not a dangerous man. He was angry last night, but he wouldn't do anything to hurt my child ...

Would he?

Detective Drisklay has his pencil poised over his notebook. "Address?"

As soon as I tell him, there's a minor whirlwind of activity. Drisklay radios the information in and asks one of his men to check on Damion to see if my son is with him even though there's no way Tyson could have gotten there on his own. Dad asks what in the world Damion and I had to fight about the same night we got engaged. At this point, Drisklay demands to know exactly when I planned to tell him that Damion was my fiancé and not just my boyfriend, and Mom's acting like she's afraid we're all in danger of disappearing into thin air if we don't eat *something*.

Meanwhile I'm thinking that the police better find my son perfectly safe and unharmed at Damion's house, and Damion better make sure he gets himself a really good lawyer and an even better bodyguard because if he's done anything to put my son in harm's way, I swear I'm going to kill him.

CHAPTER 12

The next ten minutes pass with torturous slowness while we wait to hear if Drisklay's men have found Tyson with my boyfriend. I have no idea why we aren't all piling into his squad car to look ourselves, but then again, if I were Drisklay and had control over a bunch of officers who had to do my dirty work for me, maybe I'd stay in on this cold Christmas morning, too.

Of course, whatever I know about police proceedings, it's because I've watched a few action movies and eventually ended up on the wrong side of the law.

I'm not a felon anymore, by the way. I think I already mentioned how Dad and a few others took my case and finally got that off my record. But those were some tough years, let me tell you. Even out of prison, do you know how hard life is for a woman who's spent her life enslaved to a pimp and now has a record for being an accessory to the prostitution of minors? Seriously, if you were a business owner, is that the kind of employee you would hire?

I wouldn't have even hired myself. Because even when I realized exactly what kind of person Jarrod was — exactly what he was doing to me and those other girls, some of them just as young as I'd been when I first met him and fell victim to his charm — I still went back to him.

More than once.

Which is why I worry so much about Tyson. If I kept making the same mistakes far into my twenties, how can I expect my son to ever learn anything when he's only five? How can I get him through twelve years of public education if he can't even keep from getting kicked out of preschool?

Of course, none of this matters as long as he's still missing. What's taking those cops so long to get back to us with some information?

"When should we hear something?" It's probably been less than two minutes since I last asked, but this silence is going to drive me insane.

Drisklay doesn't answer, just takes a loud sip of coffee, which by now is probably cold.

Mom's sitting by my side, rubbing my back and stroking my arm as if I were a little lost kitten she brought in from a rainstorm. I don't want her sympathy. Sympathy implies that something bad has happened, but we don't know that yet.

Maybe this is all some sort of prank. I think about a joke my dad told in church once, since that man literally can't begin a sermon with anything other than a funny story or corny Bible riddle.

This one starts with a nurse who telephones the on-call doctor to let her know that there's an emergency at the hospital. Instead of getting hold of the physician, she finds herself talking to her four-year-old son.

"Is your Mommy there?" she asks, and the little boy responds in a quiet voice, "Yes, but she can't talk right now."

"This is really important," says the nurse. "Could you go get her for me?"

"Sorry," the little boy whispers. "That would be impossible."

Feeling put out, the nurse sighs, "Well, is your dad there?"

"Yes," the boy answers, "but he can't come to the phone either."

"Why not?"

"He's busy talking to the policemen."

Thinking that the little boy might be in trouble, which could also explain why he's been whispering, the nurse asks, "Is everything all right over there?"

"No." The boy's talking so quietly, she can hardly make out his words. "Mom's crying, and the policemen are searching everywhere."

Hearing something loud in the background, the nurse asks, "What's that noise?"

"That's the helicopter. They've got their bright lights on and are flying around the whole neighborhood."

By now, the nurse is even more alarmed. "Who are they looking for?"

The little boy lets out a giggle. "Me."

I can't for the life of me remember what that story had to do with Dad's sermon, but I'm going back and forth between hoping this whole incident is Tyson's idea of a bad Christmas prank and imagining the ways I'm going to kill him if it is.

Drisklay gets a buzz on his radio. It's all in police talk, and even though I understand the individual words, I have no idea what the officer on the other end is saying. I can tell, though, from Drisklay's face that it's not good news.

He barks out a quick order, then looks at me and shakes his head. "No sign of him there. I've got one of my men questioning your boyfriend now, but my gut tells me it's a dead end, and unless we're talking about that taco truck outside the courthouse, my gut very rarely lets me down."

I have no idea if this is Drisklay's way of trying to lighten the mood. If it is, you wouldn't know it from his features, which are about as serious as what you'd see on a baseball umpire or one of those guards in those tall fuzzy hats standing in front of the Queen of England's palace.

"He wouldn't have wandered off on Christmas morning without telling us," Mom says, and I know she's right. Tyson's a pain in the butt, but he wouldn't risk skipping out on Christmas presents and stocking stuffers just to play a joke.

Dad lays a heavy hand on my shoulder. "Is this something you think Damion might be involved in?"

I shake my head. Angry as we might get at each other, as stupid as our fight was last night, Damion would never hurt my son. It would take a special sort of monster who would resort to injuring a little kid.

A special sort of monster just like the kind who would threaten to kill one of his underage girls if I didn't fix her makeup and prepare her for the work she was expected to do. Who promised to burn my parents' house down if I didn't help him get into the bank where I work.

"Do you know anyone else who could have done something like this?" Mom winces when she asks the question, and I know how much it pains her to admit that there might be some sort of foul play involved in Tyson's disappearance.

Everyone's looking at me now, even the detective with his perfectly expressionless features.

I don't want to have to say what I'm about to say, especially not with my parents listening in. Mom will get worried and turn weepy. Dad will be angry, not at me but at the memory of the felon who stole so much of his daughter's childhood. The detective, if he's anything like the other cops I talked to after Jarrod's arrest, will probably find a way to shift the blame onto me, but if that's what it's going to take to get my son back, so be it.

Bring it on.

I take a deep breath. The air in my parents' dining room turns heavy.

"There is someone who may have been involved," I confess. It's physically painful to get the words out. "His name's Jarrod. Old ex-boyfriend of mine."

I stare around the table. Am I going to say it?

Yes, I am. It could be important to this investigation.

Knowing full well what kind of drama is about to unfold, I take a deep breath, avoid my parents' eyes, and add, "He's Tyson's father."

CHAPTER 13

So that went about as well as I expected. Mom's gotten up to make more coffee, except she's only using that as an excuse to go into the other room so it's not as obvious to us all that she's crying.

Dad was so mad when I told him that Jarrod had shown up again and was making threats against me — not to mention the nice little reveal about him being Tyson's father — that he started using his more colorful swear-alternatives, which are usually reserved for skinheads, child molesters, and Communists.

Drisklay is the only one who keeps his cool, not that I could picture him being fazed by anything or anyone. He's on his little radio now, telling his men to look into the lead. Thankfully, he hasn't yelled at me for not calling the cops the second Jarrod showed up at my work. Maybe that's coming, or maybe he understands just a little bit what I've gone through.

As for me, I've given up all hope that this is some sort of game of Christmas morning hide and seek. It's not even a domestic dispute between me and Damion. No, this is a kidnapping, pure and simple. Jarrod's way of getting back at me for everything I've done.

For refusing to give him the security schedule at my bank. For ignoring his threats when he ordered me to help him and his buddy with that job of theirs. For everything that happened years ago when I let the cops into the house and then testified against him, even though my confession incriminated us both.

There are so many reasons for him to extract his revenge. Even the fact that I've moved on with my life, that I'm with someone else ...

Or at least I was until last night.

Mom's still dabbing her eyes, but she's sitting down at the table again. Dad takes her hand in his left and mine in his right. This gesture is so familiar to me, so ingrained in my upbringing, that I bow my head without thinking about it. Before I close my eyes, I see my mom reach out to take Drisklay's hand, but he makes a noisy show of clearing his throat and scooting back his chair to get himself more coffee.

While the detective fills up the childish snowman mug, Dad begins to pray for my son. Silent tears slide down my cheeks, and wordless fears pour out of my heart where all I can do is hope they find audience in the throne room of heaven.

CHAPTER 14

I swear if this detective asks me one more question about Jarrod, I'm going to scream. So far, he's wanted to know if in the past two weeks Jarrod's hit me, if he's had any contact with my son, if he's mentioned details for his plans at my bank, or if I've slept with him.

I have to laugh at this last question.

As if.

Then again, it was years after I walked away from Jarrod that I ended up pregnant with Tyson, so maybe the detective's question isn't quite as ridiculous as it sounds.

I was twenty-seven when he got out of prison the first time. Twenty-seven but still making a lot of childish mistakes. I hadn't been able to kick the drug habit yet, hard as I tried, and my track record made it basically impossible to get any sort of legitimate job. I was starving, homeless, and dying for my next fix when Jarrod found me. I was stupid and naïve. I wanted to believe he was the savior coming to rescue me from my life on the streets. Plus he had a regular supplier and plenty of cash, which feels an awful lot like love when you're as dependent as I was.

Getting pregnant with Tyson made me desperate enough to leave him, this time for good. Even so, that would have been nothing but a single good intention among hundreds if Mom and Dad hadn't managed to find me the one rehab program in the country that could help me. I'd tried so many things by then, and even today I don't know what it was about Sacred Meadows that made it work when everything else failed. By the time Tyson was born, I was clean.

Have been ever since. True story. And if that's not a testimony for you, I don't know what is.

Things might have been harder except that Sacred Meadows was way out there on the West Coast, and Jarrod had no idea where I'd gone. He didn't even know I was pregnant with his child when I left.

I moved back east so Mom could help once Tyson was born, and by then Jarrod had been arrested again. And now I'm sitting next to my parents, hating the fact that I've just told them who Tyson's real dad is. For a minute, I'm afraid that once we do find my son they're never going to see him the same way anymore, but that's ridiculous. For all the things you could fault them for, being unloving wouldn't even make the list.

Tyson's genes aren't his fault, but I'm afraid that this will somehow complicate the case, which is what I've asked the detective.

"He's not listed on the birth certificate?" Drisklay asks.

I shake my head.

"You ever get a paternity test?"

"No."

"Are you sure it's his?" Drisklay acts like we are talking about a lost jacket or lunch box and not my flesh and blood son who is missing.

"There wasn't anyone else at the time." Talk about an awkward conversation to have in front of your parents on Christmas morning. "Is that going to make things trickier?" I ask. "Legally, I mean."

Drisklay takes another noisy sip of black coffee and shakes his head. "Since there's no record, paternity would take time to prove. And since he hasn't ever been involved in the child's care, there isn't any legal ground for him to stand on."

I let out my breath. At least there's some good news in this nightmare of a day.

"Does he know the child's his?"

I actually have no idea how to answer this question. Jarrod can do simple math. All he's got to do is ask my son when his birthday is ...

I can't believe that right now, right as we speak, Tyson might be with him. After all I've done to try to protect him from his genetics, from the curse of his parental heritage. Was that all for nothing?

And what's Jarrod want with him, anyway? Drisklay's talked about setting up our phones so that if Jarrod demands some sort of ransom they can trace the call. But I'm not so convinced that blackmail's the goal. With someone like Jarrod, revenge is just as likely, which means my son might already be ...

No, I'm not going to think like that. It's Christmas. The time for miracles. If there really is a God — and of course I know that there is — he would never be cruel enough to let something so terrible happen to my son.

It would be impossible.

I think back to my parents' prayers around the table just a few minutes ago, to the faith and conviction in their voices as they praised God for all of his blessings even with my son missing. I might not be a role model for young believers or junk like that, but I guarantee you will never meet more devoted Christians than my mom and dad. Which means that God is going to answer their prayers, keep my son safe, and bring him home to me.

Or so help me, I swear I'll kill whoever's hurt him.

CHAPTER 15

There's a knock on the door. I'm so startled I literally jump in my seat and stare at the detective who's frowning at my mom.

"I should get that?" she says, half as a question and half as a statement, but she still doesn't move.

Whoever's here opens the door himself. For some reason I worry that it's Jarrod with a gun about to blow us all away. When I see the detective reach for his sidearm, I realize that maybe my imagination isn't overreacting.

"Blessing? You there?"

My mom jumps out of her chair at Damion's voice and rushes down the hall to give my boyfriend/fiancé/ex-boyfriend a hug. "Are you all right?" she asks as if we were talking about his kidnapped son and not mine.

Damion works his way past her until he's standing in front of me. "What's going on? The police came. They said Tyson's missing. Have you found him yet?"

Hearing the worry in Damion's voice makes me ashamed that anyone might have suspected him of kidnapping my boy.

"He's still missing." I can't believe those words are really coming out of my mouth. Can't believe they're true.

"It's going to be ok." He sounds so certain. So confident. Or maybe I'm just desperate enough that I have to believe him.

He gives me a hug that assures me our argument last night is forgotten, and then his voice goes hard. "Is it that guy? Have you told them about him yet?" He nods at the detective.

"They're looking into it." Now more than ever I want to throw myself against his chest and forget that any of this is real.

Mom's tugging on my dad's shirtsleeve. "Come on," she says. "Let's give the kids a little privacy. I'm sure they have a lot to talk about."

Dad frowns but gets up.

"We'll be in the bedroom if you need us." Mom straightens her hair and adjusts her bathrobe. The detective clears his throat and heads into the kitchen for more coffee.

Damion looks at me with a pained expression I doubt I'll ever forget. "I'm sorry."

There are so many things he could mean by that. As in, *I'm sorry that your son's been kidnapped. I'm sorry that I embarrassed you last night by telling your parents and everyone else you were pregnant. I'm sorry that I didn't run after you when you left home so mad.*

He gives me another hug. "I'm so sorry," he repeats, and I know him well enough to understand that he's apologizing for all these things at once.

CHAPTER 16

You've never witnessed a quieter Christmas lunch than we are having right now. True story.

The detective's left, following up with the men he sent to hunt for Jarrod.

Damion's still here, and since we've made up after our fight last night, we have very little to say to each other.

Mom keeps making half-hearted attempts to lighten the mood, which really just adds to how depressing this whole meal feels.

She clears her throat. "I'm surprised these buns didn't go stale overnight. I forgot to seal the bag."

Silence.

A few minutes later, "You know, I don't usually add sour cream to the green beans like this, but I think I'll do that from now on."

Nothing.

Dad's expression doesn't give a hint as to what he's thinking. Is he still trying to figure out how I could have stooped low enough to hook up again with Jarrod after he got out of jail that first time? Is he mad at me that I never told him who Tyson's father was?

And what does Damion make of all this? Once he realized the sort of drama I'd invited into my life, what kind of baggage I'm still carrying around from my past, however unwillingly, you'd think he'd be the first one out the door, but I know that's not the case.

It's funny. Back before last night, before we got engaged, I wondered what kind of stepdad Damion would be. Now I realize that he's acted like Tyson's father for years now. It was dumb for me to be worried about something like that.

Dumb to take Damion for granted for so long.

The fact that we've made up should be great news, except it's obviously overshadowed by everything else that's going on. If Jarrod's trying to get back at me, what's going to stop him from hurting my son?

Mom makes a far-too-chipper comment about how the ham leftovers are even better than they were last night, but her observation is met only by the sound of scraping forks.

She clears her throat. "Maybe we should pray again."

I expect Damion to bristle beside me. He's never liked how into God my family is. Says it makes him uncomfortable, like they're shoving religion down his throat, but he's the first to say what a good idea that is and bows his head.

In true Lindgren family tradition, we all hold hands, and Dad starts off our time of prayer.

"Lord, great God and heavenly Father, we give you praise for little Tyson, for what an energetic, smart, and capable young boy he is. We give you praise for the fact that you love him so much you sent your son to die on the cross to forgive all of his sins, and we know that your love is strong enough to reach him even now. So wherever he is, Lord, we pray that Tyson's soul would be kept safe and sound in your care. We pray that his spirit would be protected from all fear, that his mind would be delivered from worries.

"We know that on our own, we have no right to ask you for anything, but your Word tells us that we are co-heirs with Christ, that everything which belongs to you has been granted unto us. All your good promises in Scripture are *yes* and *amen* in our Lord and Savior Jesus Christ."

I feel movement to my left and am surprised at the way Damion is nodding his head in fervent agreement. I keep my half-opened eyes on my fiancé while Dad continues.

"And so, dear Lord, Almighty King of the universe, we lift Tyson up to you. We surrender his sweet little spirit to you. We ask, God, that you look upon us now, that you see us and know our troubles. Here we are, Lord. It's Christmas Day, but instead of rejoicing in the fact that you sent Jesus down to earth to be born and eventually become the atonement for our sins, our minds are wracked with worry. We confess our anxieties to you, Lord, each and every one, but we declare that we have not received a spirit that makes us a slave again to fear. We confess that these burdens are far too heavy for us to bear alone, yet you are the one who proclaims in your Holy Word that your load is easy and your burden is light.

"It's in your Word you tell us to cast our cares upon you because you care so deeply for us. So that's just what we're doing. We take our fears and our burdens and our uncertainties and set them at the foot of your cross in hopes that they'll be a pleasing and acceptable offering to you. We can't shoulder them on our own strength."

Damion squeezes my hand. I look over and see the tears streaking down his cheeks. I lay my head against his chest and listen to the sound of his breaking heart.

Dad's voice is powerful. He always booms when he talks, but something changes when he's praying or preaching. It's hard to explain, but it's been happening ever since I met him. His voice continues to swell with faith and conviction.

"We ask you to remind us that not even a sparrow falls to the ground apart from your will. We ask you to remind us that there is no place we can run from your presence, no place where your Spirit cannot minister to us. You know exactly where Tyson is, you know exactly what he needs right now, and we come before you with humility but also with great boldness knowing that through the blood of Christ shed on his cross we can approach your throne of grace with great confidence and full assurance."

Damion is weeping openly now. Mom is too. When my own tears threaten to fall, I'm powerless to stop them.

Only Dad's dry-eyed, and his voice is full of even more confidence.

"And so Lord, we come before you now and …"

I'm not listening anymore. I'm not paying attention to my dad's heartfelt prayer.

I'm twelve years old, nothing but a child, and Jarrod is telling me how much he loves me, how much he wants to be with me, how this terrifying pregnancy won't be enough to separate us from our love for one another.

CHAPTER 17

"Come on, baby. You don't have to cry." Jarrod holds me close against his chest. I can hear his heart beating.

So soothing. So familiar.

"They're going to find out," I whine.

"Shh." He kisses the top of my head. "Your foster parents are so busy with their real kids they're not going to notice a thing."

I shake my head. "They're not like that." How can I make him understand? How can I tell him that Carl and Sandy aren't like any of the other families I've been with?

How can I express the way for the first time in my life I'm with two people I don't want to disappoint?

"They're going to find out," I repeat. I sound like one of my grandmother's broken records. I miss her so much.

Jarrod holds me close. "How? You're scrawny as a twig. Your breasts haven't even changed."

"Why would they change?"

He laughs. "So you can nurse the kid."

As if I should have known. I don't have a clue about anything, and I tell him, "Nobody's ever told me how to nurse." The only thought I've ever given to my breasts are praying I'll eventually end up in a C or maybe even a D if God's feeling especially generous.

Jarrod's rubbing my back. "You won't have to know how to nurse because we've already decided what we're going to do, right?"

I nod.

His voice is low and soft. "You're gonna stick to the plan. We've gone over this a hundred times."

It's true. We have. But now that I'm with Carl and Sandy, now that I'm part of what feels like an actual, genuine *family*, I'm not sure I want to go through with it, and I tell Jarrod.

He laughs again. "What else are you going to do? Let them think you've been sleeping around like a little streetwalker and ask them to raise the brat?"

I don't like it when he talks like this. Like he hates the baby. I know he's right when he tells me we can't keep it, and there's no way to get rid of it now that it's the size it is, but it hurts my feelings when he acts like the baby's done something wrong. The way I see it, this pregnancy is proof of how much Jarrod and I love each other. Scared and overwhelmed as I feel, there's something special about that.

Jarrod passes me his joint. He doesn't always like to share, so I'm grateful he's in a generous mood, and I feel calmer right away. He kisses my neck. "I'm going to take care of you. I promise. Don't worry about a thing."

CHAPTER 18

Dad's done praying. So is Mom, even though I can't remember a single word she said. It's not until Damion joins our little holy bubble that I snap out of my daydream and pay attention to what's going on in the present.

"Jesus, it's me. Damion." He sounds about as awkward as he did on the phone that first time he asked me out. "So, well, we're just really worried about Tyson here, and we'd really like you to tell us where he is." He clears his throat. "I guess that's all."

I open my eyes. So do my parents. I remind myself that now is an inappropriate time to laugh, and then my dad says, "Amen," and our prayer time is finished.

We all stare at each other for several seconds before Mom finally asks, "Well, who's still hungry?"

There's a knock at the front door, but it sounds far too subdued and somber for it to be anyone delivering good news. I stay seated while Mom goes to answer it, and I get a familiar wave of nausea when I hear Detective Drisklay droning down the hall.

"We've got men looking into a few leads, but so far still no sign of Jarrod or the kid."

Damion looks at me with a pained expression. I try to avoid his gaze. I don't want to see my own pain and fear mirrored in his eyes. He wraps his arm around me. "It's all going to work out. Don't worry about a thing."

As if I hadn't heard that line before.

Mom comes up behind me. "Sweetie, the detective has a few more questions for you. I thought maybe you'd want to use the den."

It's sweet the way she's trying to protect my privacy now. Like I didn't spill out all my secrets earlier.

Then again, I didn't. I nod and get up. "You gonna be all right here?" I ask Damion. I'm grateful Mom's giving us the den. There's no way I'd tell Drisklay about the baby with my parents listening, but maybe when it's just the two of us I'll find a way to bring it up. If Jarrod's going to follow through on all his threats, I need to be ready for this one.

Mom puts a platter of pies and pastries in front of my boyfriend at the table. "We'll be just fine," she says. "You go talk to that detective and take all the time you need."

I follow Drisklay into the den. Glancing at his Styrofoam coffee cup, I wonder how much caffeine he's already had today. Is he that tired? Should he even be working on this case?

He sits down in the desk chair, the one my dad owns but never uses, and I sink into the recliner across from him. For a split second, I expect

Drisklay to say something human like, "How are you holding up?" or "Is there anything I can do for you?" but I've obviously forgotten who I'm dealing with.

"So why'd your ex think you'd help him get into this bank?"

I rub my sweaty palms on the armrests of the recliner while Drisklay stares at me. It takes all my mental focus to remind myself that I'm not the criminal here. I'm not being interrogated.

Although maybe I will be by the time this interview's up.

Drisklay's waiting for my response. I have so many reasons not to tell him the whole story. The chances of it helping him find my son are next to impossible, but I'm so afraid that the truth is going to come out in the end, it's like I'm practicing with this man I hardly know to prepare for when everyone else finds out. Trying not to imagine the expressions on my parents' faces when they discover what happened. Hoping that Damion will understand but knowing that he won't.

We've found ourselves engaged, broken up, and then back together in less than twenty-four hours, but if my secret really is exposed for everyone to see, Damion will be gone for good. I know it as clearly as I know that my parents are both saints or that I deserve to go to hell for all the horrible things I've done.

I shut my eyes for just a second, trying to figure out how I'm going to get this story out. When I'm awake, I refuse to think about it, but that doesn't stop the nightmares. I've relived this exact moment dozens, maybe hundreds, of times. Seen it play out like I'm some actress on the big screen, except the theater is my own mind and there's no way to stop the movie or get up and leave if I don't want to watch the film again.

I'm at the payphone right outside my junior high. The starting bell's about to ring. "Something's weird." I tell Jarrod what happened, and he laughs at me.

"It's not funny," I protest. "It looks like I peed my pants." It would be embarrassing to admit except so many other strange things have happened to me in the past nine months that this is just one oddity among many.

"That's what I told you to expect," Jarrod says. "And it's a good thing. It means this will all be over soon."

"Well, I need you to bring me some clean pants or something. I have a math test soon."

He chuckles on the other end of the line. "You might be missing that test, babe."

"What do you mean? I know this stuff. I actually studied for it."

"You can study for a simple math test but you don't even know when you're in labor?"

"It's not labor," I tell him. Why won't he listen to me? I don't even hurt. "All I need are clean clothes. I'm about to be late."

"It's probably best if you forget about school today."

For a minute, I'm hopeful that Jarrod's going to pick me up so we can spend some time together. It's been months since it's just been him and me. He's got this cousin, a girl around my age but we go to different schools. Mel's parents are getting a divorce, so she's having a really hard time. Jarrod's been spending most of his evenings with her. I know I shouldn't be upset about that. He's such a nice guy, and he has such a big family, and they all sort of look to him when they're going through difficulties. But childish as it sounds, I really miss him.

Unfortunately, he has no intention of picking me up and whisking me away from school.

"Listen to me carefully. All those things we talked about with the baby, they're going to start happening. It might not be right away, but don't be surprised when it does."

I can't believe what I'm hearing. For the past few months, ever since Jarrod told me what was going on, part of me thought it was all a big mistake. I've only had one period in my entire life. I'm not even a hundred pounds. All these things that he said would happen, they sounded so impossible.

In fact, they still do.

I'm trying hard not to cry. I don't want Jarrod to laugh at me again or call me a baby. "Can you come pick me up?" I ask.

He sighs. "I'm sorry, babe. Mel's got a bad earache. I might even have to take her to the doctor's."

"Can't I come with you?" I hate how squeaky and small my voice sounds. I don't know what he's thinking on the other end of the line, and I hold my breath anxiously.

"How about this. I'll get Mel ready to see the doctor now, and then you call me again right before lunch and I'll come and get you if that's still what you want."

"So I should go to class and take my test?"

There's a smile in his voice. "Sure, babe. Go to class and take your test. Make sure you get an A, all right?"

I grin in spite of how strange it feels to have my pants half soaked and something wet like pee trickling down my leg. "What about my jeans?" I ask. "Could you bring me a new pair on your way to the doctor's?"

"No, we're headed to the other side of town. I'm not going your direction."

"Oh." I try to mask the disappointment in my voice. "I know. I can ask the school nurse for a pad." I'm proud to have come up with such a good solution on my own, but Jarrod doesn't sound so enthusiastic.

"I don't want you seeing the nurse today."

"Why not?"

"We talked about it before, remember? People don't understand us. They think I'm too old for you. If they find out you're pregnant, I could get in big trouble. Maybe even go to jail."

I hate it when he talks like this. How could someone go to jail just for loving too much? It's not fair. I promise him I'll stay away from the nurse. "But you'll come and get me soon?"

"Yeah, call me after lunch like we said." The grin is back in his voice. "And good luck on your test. Make me proud."

I'm blushing by the time I hang up the payphone, but I'm only halfway toward the school building before my whole stomach feels like it's on fire. I think about turning around and begging Jarrod to come and get me now. He would, too, if I really needed him, but he's been so worried about his cousin, and Mel has problems of her own. I can't be selfish.

The fire subsides. I take a deep breath. I can do this.

The morning bell rings, but it's just the warning. I can still make it to class on time if I hurry. Thankfully, I'm wearing dark jeans. I pray no one gets close enough to notice the wet stains. Jarrod doesn't want me talking to the nurse, but maybe I can find one of my friends who has a pad with her that I can use. I hurry up. I have a math test this morning, and I don't want to be late.

CHAPTER 19

The last ten minutes have been pure torture, and the detective's expressionless face isn't giving me any sort of clues about whether telling him everything was the right thing or not.

He looks mad. It's hard to know why I feel that way because he's always got something of a scowl, but instead of looking bored like usual, he seems angry.

Angry at who? At me for what I did?

Or angry at Jarrod for putting a junior-higher through such torment?

Jarrod told me to call him at lunch, but I couldn't wait that long. I made it through my math test, but by English my stomach hurt so bad I thought I might throw up. Even the teacher noticed something was wrong, asked if I wanted to visit the nurse, but what twelve-year-old girl would willingly get her boyfriend thrown into jail simply because adults can't understand how a man his age could fall in love with someone as young as twelve?

I tried catching him again after third hour, but he didn't pick up. I wish I had asked him the name of Mel's doctor. For a minute, I thought about calling Sandy and telling her everything, but there was Jarrod's voice in the back of my head reminding me that no other grown-up could understand the kind of love we had for one another.

We'd talked about the delivery before. Had it all planned out. The only problem was I never expected it to happen while I was in school, and if it did I figured that Jarrod would drop everything and come and get me.

What was taking him so long?

I didn't want to leave a message on his answering machine because I had to save my coins. I'd let it ring three times, hang up, collect my returned money, then try again, each time praying the call would go through.

Finally the pain grew so bad that I went back into the school, resolved to talk to the nurse, but the closer I got to the office, the louder I could hear Jarrod's voice in my head. *They won't understand us. They'll think I'm some sort of pervert. They'll send me to jail. We'll never be allowed to see each other again.*

With tears stinging my cheeks, I made my way to the bathroom where I waited until the lunch bell rang. Then I dragged myself back outside, back to that stupid phone booth. At least this time God answered my prayers, and Jarrod picked up.

"Hello?"

"It's me." It wasn't just my stomach now that hurt but my back too, and I scarcely had the breath to get more than a few words out at a time.

Jarrod's tone was full of cocky cheerfulness. "Hey, babe. How'd your test go?"

"My tummy hurts." I wiped my eyes, resolved not to let him know I was crying.

His voice was full of sympathy. "That's what I told you was gonna happen. But don't worry. Like I said before, this will all be over soon, and then things can go back to the way they used to be."

Used to be? I didn't know what he was talking about. Had there ever been a time when I wasn't pregnant and terrified and in so much pain?

"Are you gonna come get me?" When he didn't answer right away, I felt compelled to remind him, "It's lunchtime."

He sighed. "Gee, babe, I'm really sorry, but the doctor put Mel on some pretty heavy antibiotics. She's got a bad ear infection. High fever too. I can't leave her alone right now."

"Can't she come with you?"

He lowered his voice. "I hate to say it, babe, but I think she's a little jealous of you. With her parents getting divorced and all, I hate asking her to spend too much time around the two of us together. Seeing how in love we are just reminds her of how bad things are with her folks, you know?"

The fire in my abdomen took my breath away for several seconds, and when I could finally speak again, I couldn't hide my sob. "It hurts really bad."

"I know, babe. Some people in your situation would be acting really selfish right now. They wouldn't be thinking about Mel, her ear infection, or how hurt her feelings are about her parents. I swear you're the sweetest girl I've ever loved."

"I'm the only girl you've ever loved," I reminded him, and he laughed.

"Course you are."

"Lunch is over in about half an hour," I said. "Think you could get me then?"

"Yeah, I could do that. I'll pick you up by the bus stop."

I didn't want to tell him that with as bad as I felt, I wasn't even sure I could walk that far. I was just relieved to know he'd be coming for me.

"Ok. I'll go over now and just wait for you."

"Know what? Maybe you should head back to school. I might be a little late, that's all. Don't want you standing out in the cold."

As if that wasn't what I was already doing talking to him on the payphone.

"How will I know when you get here?" I asked.

"I'll sign you out at the office," he said, and then added with a chuckle, "Remember, you're my niece."

"Not technically."

"Yeah, but nobody else has to know that. So head back to school, and wait for me to get you. All right?"

"Ok." Did he hear the disappointment in my voice?

"One more thing. If it gets real bad, or things start to happen real fast before I show up, you remember the plan, don't you?"

As far as I knew, the plan was for Jarrod to pick me up so we could walk through this together.

Without giving me the chance to respond, he said, "All right, Mel's about to get up from her nap now, and I promised to heat her up some soup. So hang in there, and I'll talk to you real soon."

Said the man who had no intention of picking me up from school in half an hour or any time that day.

CHAPTER 20

I've told Drisklay everything, and now the silence is too much for me to handle. "Am I in trouble?" I ask.

"For being the twelve-year-old victim of statutory rape?" He raises an eyebrow, the closest thing to an expression I've seen on his face all day. "No."

"What about ..." I clear my throat. "What about the other stuff?"

He waves his hand in the air. Does that mean he doesn't want to talk about it? Should I be worried? Do I need a lawyer?

"So last week Jarrod told you that unless you helped him with this bank heist, he'd hurt your family and tell everyone what you just told me?"

Ignoring the lump in my throat, I nod.

"And nobody else knows this story?"

I shake my head, and he lets out a low whistle like he's impressed at something.

I finally muster up the courage to ask, "Is it going to help you find my son?"

He shrugs. "I don't see how."

Great. I've just confessed to this detective what I've never had the guts to share with my parents, my fiancé, any sort of counselor or therapist or pastor, and he's saying it doesn't even matter.

I picture leaning into this reclining chair until it swallows me up forever.

Drisklay meets my eye. Holds my gaze in his. At first, I'm moved enough to expect some word of kindness or compassion, but all he says is, "You know, some people would blame you for what you did."

I stare into my lap. As if he had to tell me.

"The way I see it, the real criminal in this case was the baby's father."

I can't look up. Can't meet his gaze again. I'm already so close to crying I have to bite my lip.

"I'm not saying you did the right thing," he adds, as if I ever had any doubts. "I'm just saying if it were my daughter in your situation, after I killed the thug who did those things to her, I'd tell her that I understood how someone so young and vulnerable could make that kind of terrible mistake."

If he's trying to lessen my sense of guilt, I'm not sure it's working. The tears stream down my cheeks. Drisklay passes me a box of tissues, tosses his empty Styrofoam cup into the trash, and walks out of the den.

CHAPTER 21

Mom's bending over me, clucking assurances and trite words of comfort that do nothing to take away my shame and remorse.

Much as I realize the detective was trying to offer me an escape from my guilt, I know he's wrong.

There are some things that maybe I didn't have much choice about. The fact that when I was sixteen Jarrod dragged me to an abortion clinic when I got pregnant with his child for the second time. Or agreeing to work a double shift because that eleven-year-old he'd just brought into the stable kept crying so hard she couldn't work. What else could I do? It was either that or watch her forced onto the streets where she probably would have hyperventilated from fear.

But that day at school, the day I went into labor with Jarrod's baby, I had every choice in the world.

I could have walked into the nurse's office. Do you know how many times I set my mind to stumble out of the bathroom stall where I'd locked myself in and tell her everything? When the bell rang and I realized school was over and Jarrod still hadn't come to pick me up, I could have gone home to Carl and Sandy. Let them know what was happening. I could have found a teacher, the principal, anyone.

Instead, I stayed in that stall long past the afternoon bell, into the evening when the halls filled once more with everyone who'd come to watch the boys' basketball game.

It was around that time I stopped wondering how scared Carl and Sandy must have felt when I didn't come home after school. All I could think was *Please, God. Help.*

I hadn't grown up in the church, but in between my mom taking off with some lifeguard half her age and me starting my journey in the foster system, I lived with my grandma. She was this old-school Christian who made me memorize all kinds of Bible verses, forbid any kind of talking or wiggling in church, the works. So I believed in God by the time I had locked myself into the bathroom stall, believed in him enough to beg him to have mercy on me and make this nightmare end.

Why hadn't Jarrod come? He'd promised. I'd waited in my classes for as long as I could, every minute expecting one of the office assistants to stop by with a note excusing me for the rest of the day. Eventually, the pain and fear were so bad I went to the bathroom and didn't come out, but I figured if Jarrod wanted to find me he could page me over the PA system.

Where was he?

We had a plan. A plan that sounded grotesque and terrifying but a plan that Jarrod promised to carry out for me. We were in it together. How many times had he told me that while pledging his eternal love? I thought through what he told me a few hours earlier when I called him on the payphone. *If it gets real bad, or things start to happen real fast before I get there, you remember the plan, don't you?*

Yes. I remembered. The plan was for Jarrod to be right there with me, explain everything that was happening, help me through the discomfort and the fear and the tearing, and then he was going to do the rest.

You remember the plan, don't you?

Had he known he wouldn't be here? No. That wasn't like him. He had a good reason. Maybe Mel was even sicker. Maybe she was in the hospital. Jarrod loved me. He knew how much I needed him, and the fact that we were apart was as painful and traumatic for him as it was for me.

That's what he told me at midnight when I took the city bus from school to his place. Mel was there, looking quite recovered from whatever infection she'd had, probably thanks to the miracle of antibiotics and Jarrod's TLC. But as soon as he saw me, he told Mel to get lost and spent the entire night and the whole next day holding me, kissing me, telling me how proud he was.

"You did what we talked about, didn't you?"

"Yeah," I told him, starved as I was for his approval. "I remembered the plan."

Another kiss. Dozens of kisses. "Good girl."

He didn't know the whole truth. He still doesn't. But that doesn't matter.

He knows enough that if he wants to ruin my life even more than he already has, he just has to tell my story to the world.

CHAPTER 22

This monotony of waiting is even more difficult than the earlier stages of panic and worry. Why hasn't the detective given us any more information? He's out again. No word when he'll be back. It's getting later in the afternoon now. If Tyson were here, I'd make him take a nap. Not that he'd sleep, but it's that time of day when I find myself in need of some peace and quiet.

Which is why when Damion asks me if I want to go on a walk around the neighborhood, I grab my shoes.

"You'll call if you hear anything," I say, and my parents promise they will.

So with cell phones in hand, Damion and I venture outside. It's cold, but not as bad as some

Christmases I remember. Not much snow. Gray and dreary, really. A fitting backdrop for this chapter in my life.

"You're quiet," Damion comments, and I wonder just what sort of conversation he expects me to have while my son's still missing. "You thinking about Tyson?"

I suppose he's just trying to fill the silence, but seriously. How dumb can you be?

"Just worried," is all I say.

"Yeah, me too." And I'm grateful because if today's shown me anything besides my own heinous guilt it's that Damion loves my son. He'll make a really good stepdad. If he'll still have me once he discovers what I've done.

For a fraction of a second, I wonder if I should tell him. If somehow hearing it from me now will make things easier later. But I'm still holding onto hope that the detective will find my son, arrest Jarrod, and my secrets will stay safe.

Damion holds my hand. I don't even think about it really. As if I could be dreaming of romance with everything else going on, Tyson missing plus all my memories of those wasted years — wasted decades if we're going to be honest — spent with Jarrod. Convinced he was the one for me. Certain I couldn't manage to live my life without him. Telling myself I needed to keep him from getting mad at me because he knew my secret, or at least he thought he did.

And now he has the power to destroy my life. If he hurts Tyson, what do I have to keep on living for? And if he lets everyone know about that baby, I'll lose the love and support of my parents and my boyfriend. Or should I call him my fiancé again? I don't even know, but we'll have time to sort that out later. After Jarrod's arrested, Tyson's returned, and my secret's buried and safe.

"That was really cool of your parents to pray for him like that," Damion says.

"Yeah."

"They're neat folks."

"Yeah."

"I wish my parents had been like that growing up."

"Yeah."

He's silent for a while, but I'm so lost in thought I hardly notice. My mind's jumped ahead to when I was sixteen. Still living with Carl and Sandy, except by then they'd adopted me and I called them Mom and Dad. Still certain that Jarrod was the only man who would ever love me, even though at that point he was sharing me with his druggie friends and making me walk the streets whenever money got tight. In spite of everything, I didn't consider myself a prostitute. I didn't do it every night or even every week. Sometimes months went by where I wouldn't work at all. Besides, to be a prostitute, you had to have a pimp or madam, and I didn't. When Jarrod was arrested the first time and the guy from the state told me what he'd been charged with, I laughed. Jarrod was a lot of things. Drug dealer. Addict.

Cheater, womanizer, and abuser. But he wasn't a pimp.

Because if he was a pimp, what would that make me?

I dropped out of school when I found out I was pregnant again. Went on to get my GED, but that wouldn't be until over a decade later. I didn't want Jarrod to find out I was pregnant. I was so afraid he'd make me relive the trauma I'd gone through in the girl's bathroom at my junior high. But there was no way to keep my secret from him.

Mom and Dad were all anti-abortion at the time (still are, by the way), and they'd talked about it enough at home and showed me those gruesome pictures and gory descriptions that I put up a pretty decent fight when Jarrod tried to take me to the clinic. I even threatened to tell the people there about the difference in our ages, remembering how scared he'd been of going to prison when I was younger.

But all it did was make him laugh. He said the age of consent was sixteen. (I found out later that he was lying, by the way. According to state law, he was so much older than I was that he still could have done prison time, but where would I have learned that? It's not like Google was around and I could just type it into my computer browser.)

So that was my first loss in the battle against having an abortion, a procedure I was sure would guarantee my soul's eternal condemnation.

When I continued to fight, he took to threatening my family (which I was used to by then), and then he said he'd tell my parents about the baby I delivered back in junior high. If I'd been thinking clearly, I would have realized that telling my folks our dirty little secret was the very last thing Jarrod would have dreamed of doing until he was safe and protected by those statute of limitation clauses.

Again I ask you, where would I have gone to learn all this junk? Scared of my parents finding out about that baby and so worried about what their uppity church friends would say about my current pregnancy, I ran away. It wasn't my first time leaving my mom and dad's, but I had never abandoned Jarrod before. You don't even want to know where I went or who I stayed with or what I did to get by, but two months later I was so shaken and battered and traumatized that I ran right back to Jarrod. Pleaded with him to forgive me for being so stubborn, begged him to take me to the clinic so I could correct my mistakes and prove how much I loved him.

There's a common assumption that abortion is this giant eraser that simply wipes away the consequences of your past and gives you a fresh start. And maybe that's how it is for some women, but as soon as I left the clinic with Jarrod, I realized that what I'd done was just as evil as what happened in that junior high bathroom. There was no way I could go home and face my parents after that, and I told Jarrod so.

He was happy to find us a place far from their prying eyes. Happy to have me all to himself without any school schedules or curfews preventing me from being his round-the-clock slave. Happy to get me even more dependent on the drugs and chemicals I could no longer function without. People sometimes talk about their lives turning into a spiral. In my case, it wasn't even that complicated. It was a free fall, no tailspin, just a straight plunge with a terrible crash at the end.

Eventually, I went back home, crawling on my hands and knees, at least figuratively. Begged my parents to forgive me for leaving them, experiencing the same sense of regret and remorse I felt when I first returned to Jarrod. Submitted to my family's rules and oversight like I had so recently surrendered my will to his. Trading one kind of oppression in for another. That's how I saw it. I was stupid, my brain so mixed up from the drugs and the trauma and from Jarrod himself, but I honestly thought my parents' home was too confining. Thought I was old enough to make decisions on my own. And that's how I began my years as a human yo-yo, bouncing from home to Jarrod to the streets and back to my mom and dad again. In between those phases were different rehab and detox programs my parents wanted me to try, but like I already mentioned, I wouldn't find my deliverance from the drugs until I was well into my twenties and pregnant (again) with Jarrod's child.

I sigh. All Damion and I have been doing for the past ten minutes is walking by the six houses in my parents' *cul de sac* then turning around and going back. My eyes stay glued to the front door in case Mom comes out with news, even though I know it would be faster for her to call my cell if she had something to say.

Damion's struck up a few conversations, or at least he's tried to. Can't blame the poor soul. He's asking questions about prayer and my parents' faith, but I'm still stuck in these painful memories. What kind of mother am I? I abandon one baby in a junior-high bathroom, let my boyfriend talk me into aborting my second, and lose my third when I'm not watching.

I still don't know how Jarrod got my son out of the house. Technically, I still don't know that Jarrod's involved at all, but it's the assumption everyone, including the detective, is working with. I think about some of the darker chapters in the Psalms and wonder if it's appropriate to pray for God to smite my ex, dash his head against the rocks, all that junk. It's something I could ask my dad, but I'd rather go on not knowing I'm sinning by praying this way.

Ignorance of the law, right?

That's something weird about God's forgiveness. I mean, I've done terrible things. That comes as no surprise. Some of the worst things a human being — a mother — can do, I've done to the children I was supposed to love and cherish and protect. But I can still go to church and hear my dad preach and feel all warm and squishy when he says that God can forgive even the worst of sinners.

So what's that mean for someone like Jarrod? That all he has to do at the end of his life is bow his head and close his eyes and say *Dear God, I'm a sinner, please forgive me*? Then he'll get into heaven? This man who pimped out fifty or sixty girls or more during his career, most of us well underage?

This demon-spawn who's kidnapped my son and has done heaven knows what to him by now could ask for forgiveness, and God would have the audacity to welcome him into paradise? I can't even.

So that's where I get caught up on this whole idea of grace. We all want it for ourselves, but what's that mean for our enemies? And I'm not just talking about the loudmouth gossip who starts some dumb rumor about you that people will only believe if they're stupider than she is. I'm talking about the man who might at this exact moment be torturing my child, or preparing to …

No, I won't go there. "Come on," I tell Damion, "I'm getting cold. Let's go back inside."

We turn around and head back, but then Damion stops when his phone rings. My heart skips but only for a second. If it was Mom or Dad or the detective, they'd be calling me.

"Hello?"

Damion's eyes widen, and then his entire face sets in a scowl. He's not saying anything.

What? I strain my neck, hoping to see his screen. He turns his back to me, still silent.

What is it?

He ends with "Ok." That's all he says before he hangs up.

"Who was that?" I ask.

Damion shakes his head. "Tell you later."

"No, you tell me now."

He sets his jaw. "Later." He grabs me by the arm.

"What are you doing? Let go of me." I don't know why he's rushing. I don't like the intensity in his expression or the strength of his grip. What's going on?

"Get in the car," he tells me when we reach my parents' driveway.

"Why? Where are we going?"

"Just get in the car," he says. "I'm telling your parents we're headed to the store."

"It's Christmas."

"Just do what I say."

I'm not used to Damion talking to me like this. I get into the passenger side of our car, my body trembling but not from the cold.

Half a minute later, he comes out the front door of my mom and dad's house, gets in, and starts up the engine.

"Tell me what's going on, or I'm getting out right now." My voice is strong. Resolute.

He sighs. "That was Jarrod on the phone. He knew your cell would be tapped, so he called mine. He wants us to meet him at this address in the North End. He's bringing Tyson with him."

CHAPTER 23

So many thoughts are spinning around in my brain that it's quite possibly about to explode. Either that or I'm going to burst Damion's eardrums with all of my questions.

"Did you talk to Tyson?"

"Did he say where they were?"

"Do you know what he wants?"

Damion clutches the steering wheel. His voice is steady, but the veins are bulging out of his forearms. "All he said was not to bring the police and come, just the two of us."

There's something fishy about this whole thing. Maybe it's how he's glancing at me out of the corner of his eye or the way he's cleared his throat three or four times.

"That's what he said? Just you and me?"

Damion deflates. "No. He said no cops, told me Tyson would get hurt if we let the authorities know what was going on."

"Ok." I wait for whatever else he hasn't told me yet, certain he doesn't want to get it out. Is my son injured? Am I going to the North End to pick up his crumpled, battered body? "What else?" I can't handle not knowing. Anything would be less torturous than this.

"He wants you to meet him there alone. I'm supposed to park the car three blocks away, give you directions, and just wait."

I sigh with relief. "That's all?" Why couldn't he have told me that from the beginning?

"You're not going to meet this guy alone."

I scoff. "Oh, yes I am." What Damion doesn't seem to remember is that it's my son's life on the line, not his. My son's captor says show up alone, unarmed, and without a single policeman in the state who knows where I'm headed? Fine. That's exactly what I'm going to do.

Damion coughs awkwardly. "I think maybe we should call that detective. He'll want to know what's going on."

"You touch your phone, I swear I'll make you drive this car right off the road."

He must sense that I'm serious because he doesn't react. I reach into his pocket and pull out his cell. "And don't think about calling anyone once I get out of the car either. You don't know this guy like I do. We're doing this his way."

He lets out his breath. "Whatever you say."

I glance at his phone, look at his most recent call. It's from a blocked number, of course. No helpful information.

I still can't figure out why Jarrod wants us out here. If it had something to do with the bank, wouldn't he demand to meet there? Now that I think about it, wouldn't Christmas Day be the perfect time to pull off a heist? Streets are empty, security's probably nothing but skeleton staff and workers with lower seniority.

So why are we going all the way out to the North End?

"What exactly did he say on the phone?" I've asked this same question multiple times, but Damion doesn't seem to understand that I want the transcript of what he heard, not the summary.

"He said I should park in front of some whole foods warehouse, wait there, and you're supposed to go three blocks down ..."

"Don't tell me the directions," I bark. "Tell me the words. Pretend I'm you and you're him and talk to me just like he talked to you. Use the same words."

"I don't remember the words."

I want to scream in frustration. He can remember directions like *whole foods warehouse* and *three blocks down*, but he doesn't know what was actually said to him? How am I supposed to know what Jarrod wants? How am I supposed to be prepared to help my son?

I'm not bothered that Jarrod wants me to come alone. I just hope my boyfriend doesn't decide to audition for superhero of the year and try to save me. I know how to handle Jarrod, don't I?

As we drive through the deserted streets, I think about the raid, the one that got Jarrod arrested the first time. It was just a few weeks after I turned eighteen, unfortunate timing since the cops and people from the state made such a big deal about how I was an adult living in a home full of prostituted minors. It's true I was the oldest of Jarrod's workers, and he often relied on me to prep the younger ones, let them know what was expected of them. Sometimes I had to be pretty harsh. They were scared of me. They didn't know it was for their own good. If I didn't get them ready and up to Jarrod's standards, he'd beat us both. What these girls didn't see is all the times I accepted the brunt of Jarrod's anger so he wouldn't take it out on them. I was especially careful to protect the preteens as much as possible.

Unfortunately, protecting them sometimes meant I had to rough them up. What would life be like for them in the stable if everyone at home treated them like royalty and then they had to go out and face the customers? Jarrod was one of the more well-meaning pimps, if such a thing exists. He'd keep tabs on the customers who beat you too bad, and as long as you stayed on his good side, he wouldn't make you go back to them a second time. Looking back, it's strange how all of us in the stable — sister-wives we sometimes called each other — were connected. On the one hand, each one of us had been told, sometimes on a daily basis and sometimes for years, that Jarrod loved us, that we were the most important person in his life, that as soon as we helped him earn enough money, he'd move us to a mansion in Hawaii or San Francisco or Paris or wherever it was we wanted to go, where we'd spend the rest of our lives in romantic bliss, just the two of us. So you can guess the ways in which we were all trying to outdo one another, prove our love to our captor.

And you can guarantee he took advantage of that situation. "Who wants to party with the guys down at the construction site?" he'd ask, and we'd all either experienced firsthand or heard rumors about how rough that crowd was. So he'd look at you and say, "What about you, Blessing?" and if you didn't act like he'd just done you the biggest favor in the world by singling you out, if you went so far as to roll your eyes or sigh or mention how bruised and beat up you'd gotten last time, he'd put his arms around your sister-wife and talk sweet to her, like, "That's ok if Blessing wants to be a little spoiled princess, isn't it, because at least I can always count on my girl Mel, can't I?"

But then he'd be gone, out expanding his network or grooming his next victim. He always seemed to have four or five girls he was working at the same time, courting them, swearing his undying love, making them trust him before he sealed the deal and moved them into our stable. And at that point, we'd welcome the newcomer with as much sensitivity and compassion as one battered woman could offer another. Of course, a few of the sister-wives were mean and stayed that way the entire time I knew them, but for the most part we all pulled together, especially when Jarrod was away.

Eventually, all of Jarrod's illegal activities caught up to him. The cops had been following him for a while but took their sweet time making a move. I guess they needed to be sure they had enough evidence to stick, otherwise all they'd do is warn him off, he'd move us all or start a new stable somewhere else, and where would be the justice in that? Still, I wish the cops could have swarmed the house a few months earlier when I was still underage, when I would have been guaranteed to be viewed as a victim and not an accessory.

Too late to change the past though, isn't it?

BLESSING ON THE RUN

It was summer. I remember because we were earning enough money for Jarrod by then — I think there were fourteen or fifteen of us together at the time — that he'd moved us into a pretty nice house. Four-bedroom. Big hot-water tank so we didn't have to ration our shower schedule all the time. Problem was the AC wasn't working, and Jarrod was stressed out about this boxing match coming to town, and he was trying to get together enough girls for a huge party, so he didn't want to spend any extra expense fixing it.

We were all lazy that afternoon. It was probably only two o'clock. Some of us were just waking up. Others had been awake, but we hadn't really done anything with our day yet. Jarrod had just gone out. Who knows where to? None of us thought to ask, either. He came when he wanted, he left when he wanted, and he took whichever one of us he wanted. Looking back, maybe that's why we were so lazy, not just because of the heat. We'd literally lost the ability to think or make choices for ourselves.

I'm the one who saw the man outside the window. He looked at me and put his finger over his mouth like he wanted me to be quiet. His eyes were kind. To this day, I can recall the compassion in his expression. Like he knew everything I'd gone through. Like he wanted to help me.

He kept his finger to his lips until I nodded and showed him I understood. He pointed to the back door. Could I meet him?

I shrugged. Jarrod would probably be gone for hours, busy as he was with the whole fight prep. So I told one of my sister-wives I was going to get a little fresh air, and I met the man out the back.

He was shorter than I expected. He put his fingers to his lips again and led me several houses down. Given my profession at the time, you might think I expected him to be a client, but I was certain he wasn't. I knew how to spot a customer. They don't make eye contact, especially not with such tenderness in their gazes.

So I wasn't scared of him. I was slightly worried about being caught, but our home was in a neighborhood with lots of alleyways, and I didn't think anyone from the house could see me.

"I'm Dominic. I'm here with the police department," the man told me, but his eyes stayed calm and gentle, so I didn't freak out too much. "I don't want to get you in trouble," he added. To this day I think he meant it. I seriously think he expected the legal system to treat me like it did the other minors who got rescued that night. If he thought I was a criminal, he wouldn't have spoken with so much compassion.

Dominic explained that they knew about Jarrod and how he was keeping us locked in his house. I had to correct him there. We were all free to leave. Any one of us. The doors were never locked from the outside. The windows never barred to prevent our escape. What held us there were chains far more wicked and significantly stronger. Some of us stayed because we honestly thought Jarrod loved us. Others refused to run away because of all the threats about what he'd do to us or our families if we tried.

Then there were girls like me whose reasons involved a sick and pathetic combination of both. Dominic and I talked for five or ten minutes while he explained what he wanted me to do. Pull down the shades in the upstairs window when I got home, then raise it back up after Jarrod was in bed.

"He sometimes doesn't sleep until three or four in the morning," I warned.

"That's ok," Dominic answered. "We'll be patient."

And that's all. He didn't ask me to unlock any doors, give him any security codes, nothing. Just pull up the blinds once Jarrod was asleep.

I guess I gave some important intel too. Which room was his, where the bed was in relationship to the door, where all the girls slept. I answered each and every question like I was hypnotized. Maybe I was. Dominic's voice was so soothing and kind. He was the first man in my life besides Carl who looked at me like I was a real person.

When we finished talking, right as I was about to turn away and go home, he set his hand on my shoulder. I couldn't believe this cop was actually touching me. "Can I ask you a question?"

I shrugged. "Sure."

"How did you get here? I mean, how did things end up like this for you?"

His expression was so pained and earnest, or else I might have laughed in his face, but he acted like he genuinely wanted to know.

I sighed. Should I tell him about my stepcousin, Jarrod's niece who introduced me to him when I was all of ten years old? I couldn't tell him about the baby, about the secret that had bound me to him from the time I was in junior high.

The cop's question haunted me as much as his eyes.

I didn't have a single word to give him in reply.

CHAPTER 24

We're at the North End now. I hate this part of town. All wharves and warehouses and industrial zones. There are so many tall buildings looming around us, Jarrod could have snipers hidden in two dozen different windows.

Or maybe I've just watched too many action movies.

Damion parks the car. "You sure you want to do this?" he asks. "Alone?"

I nod. Now that we're here, I think I could recognize my fear if I looked hard for it, but a mom will do anything for her kid, right?

At least, that's how it would be in an ideal world. Moms in an ideal world wouldn't abandon their babies in trash cans or let their boyfriends talk them into going to abortion clinics. Of course, in an ideal world, deranged ex-boyfriends wouldn't kidnap innocent children to start with, but that's beside the point.

Damion takes my hand in his. "I love you," he says. "You know that, don't you?"

What's he doing? He's acting like he'll never see me again. Does he seriously think this is goodbye? Poor fool's watched even more action movies than I have. I give him a quick peck on the cheek. "Be back soon."

"Wait." He tightens his grip. "There's something I want to do first." He's staring at my hand, and for a second I'm afraid he wants to put my engagement ring back on. Like I said, horrible sense of timing. But that's not it. "Before you go …" He clears his throat. If this is a new nervous habit he's picked up, I'll have to invest in some earplugs or something if we're going to stay together. "I was just thinking … Your parents pray all the time, right? So maybe, I don't know, maybe we could do something like that now."

I let out my breath. "Fine." I don't know why I'm being a drama queen about it. Maybe because now that we're here, I just want to find my son, take him with me, and go. But if Damion's got the itch to pray, who am I to stop him? "You gonna start or should I?"

He's blushing. My boyfriend is literally blushing. "I don't really know what to say. It's sort of ..."

"Fine," I huff, and I race through a quick prayer. I'm not even thinking about the words. It's just *help us get Tyson back, please keep us all safe, blah, blah, blah.* I finish with *amen* and figure we're done, but then Damion assumes it's his turn.

"Hey, God. I'm real sorry I never learned how to do this too good when I was growing up, but I've seen the way Blessing's parents talk to you and think that once we become a family, it's what I want to learn to do better. And teach Tyson to do better too, since maybe if he learns to pray like his grandparents do, maybe he won't get into all that trouble at school. Think that's ok to say?"

It takes me a second to realize he's directing this question at me, so I nod my head and let him get back at it. The sooner he finishes up, the sooner I can find my son.

"And well, I think that it's pretty neat hearing things about you at Christmas. It's not stuff I've thought about before."

I can't even. Is he going to just ramble on all day?

"But you know, last night me and Carl got to talking, and a lot of what he said made sense. How we've all done things we're ashamed of but you can forgive us when we ask you."

Yup, that's exactly what he's planning to do.

"So anyway, there's lots of things I guess I need you to forgive me for. Like when I lie and say I don't got any small bills on me and can't make change for my deliveries. Or when I go out with my buddies and have a few too many. And then that time when I …"

I can't even. "Tell you what," I snap, "you finish talking to God here. I'm going to go get my son back."

"Wait," he says, "you sure you don't want me to ask God to protect you? I was getting to that, you know. It's just your dad made it out like the forgiveness stuff had to happen first, and I wanted to do it all in the right order."

"I'm sure it's fine either way." I have no idea if what I've just said is biblically accurate or not, but I don't care. I make sure I've got both phones in my pocket, his and mine, I glance around to make sure I know which way I'm supposed to go, and I plow ahead, ready to find my son.

CHAPTER 25

Three blocks later, I see the old billboard where I'm supposed to make a left. It's hard to describe how I feel. I guess I thought by now I'd be more afraid, but there's something fierce in me. The mama bear that's been awakened.

Jarrod better not have laid a finger on my boy. Not if he wants to live to see the sun set this Christmas.

I follow the instructions I got from Damion. My heart's pounding but not with fear. It's like I've just finished an intense workout, except I'm not tired. I'm high on adrenaline. Adrenaline and the certainty that my son is nearby. I'll see him soon.

There's a car ahead. Is that where I'm supposed to go? I realize now that the directions didn't say. Did Damion forget to tell me the last part?

The door to the car opens. I hear someone calling for me. "Mommy!"

The baby I'm pregnant with jumps a little. I'm going to take that movement of life as a sign from God that everything's going to be ok. Didn't that happen in the Bible too? Some baby dancing in his mother's womb and that's how she knew Jesus would be the Savior or something like that? Don't ask me the details, but I'm pretty sure it's in there. Part of the Christmas story, right?

There's Tyson, just twenty or thirty feet ahead of me. I could collapse from relief to see that he's on his own two feet. It's all ok. Everything is going to be fine. I want to run toward him, but I slow myself down. All those action movies have taught me there's a ceremony to these kinds of trade-offs, if that's what you can call this, since I have no idea what I'm going to be expected to offer in exchange for my son.

Whatever the deal is, I'll take it. I've already decided. If Jarrod wants me to tell him every single piece of information I have about the bank, the security system, the workers' schedule, the safes, the lockup procedures, I'll give him everything. Let the police deal with him later. Just as long as I get my son back now. Just as long as Tyson doesn't get hurt.

"You ok, baby?" I call out to my boy, and he nods, but there's no smile on his face. Like he's not really seeing me.

There's Jarrod, his hand on my son's shoulder. I give him a nod. In this type of situation, I know he wants me to show him respect.

"I'm glad you called me," I say.

"I didn't call you," Jarrod spits, and my son flinches when he curses at me.

It's ok, baby, I want to tell him. *Trust me, that man has called me far worse.*

"You gonna let me have my son?"

Jarrod shrugs. "I wanna talk to you first."

"Can we talk a little closer?" I shout. He takes several steps forward, his hand still on Tyson's shoulder. As they come toward me, I can see how tight his grip is on my boy.

Tyson's just a few feet away now. If I reach out my fingers and he does the same, we could touch. But neither of us make a move. *Good boy.* He knows to let Jarrod feel like he's in control. I told you that kid was smart.

"You sure you're ok?" I ask Tyson again, and he nods without expression.

"Shut up," Jarrod snarls at me, so I wait for him to be the next to talk. He glances around. Is he making sure I came alone? Or does he have backup hidden in those buildings that loom so tall around us? Do I even want to know?

I blink. Count my breaths. Instead of fear or even ferocity, everything now is a haze. All my thoughts are floating in a mist, a mist that won't clear until Tyson is safe with me and we're far from the North End, far from his father and speeding home to celebrate Christmas with my folks.

Did you hear that, God? That's all I want. It's not so much to ask.

Jarrod clears his throat. "Haven't hurt the boy," he says, and I thank him politely. Like he's done me some huge favor.

Then again, he has. I'm so relieved to see my baby safe I don't care what Jarrod's done in the past or what he's planning to do in the future. *Just give me my boy and let me take him home.*

"He's actually a pretty tough kid," Jarrod says almost appreciatively. I glance at my son, whose expression hasn't changed.

That's my boy. I don't want him to get a big head. Don't want him thinking that the praise of monsters like his dad is anything worth feeling proud about.

My eyes are still on Jarrod's hand, the one that's squeezing my son's shoulder. "What do you want?" I finally ask.

He takes a step forward. I try my hardest not to flinch.

"Nothing," he answers. "Just hoping we could talk."

I try to sound casual. "I'm listening. So talk."

He frowns like he's hurt. "Come on, babe. Why you gotta be like that? Why you gotta be so cold?"

"You kidnapped my son," I remind him.

Jarrod chuckles. "That was nothing. Kid and I were bonding. Little father-son time never hurt nobody."

So he knows. I glance at Tyson to see his reaction. He doesn't look surprised. Did Jarrod already tell him? I want to know what my baby thinks, but it's like he's shut down. Not that I can blame him. If I were able to turn off my brain and just get through these next few minutes without feeling a single thing, don't you think I would?

"You had your father-son time," I say. "Now he's coming with me to spend Christmas with his family."

Jarrod winces. I've said the wrong thing. I hold my breath, wondering if he'll explode or not. This is the part I hated most when I was with him. The uncertainty. The waiting. Like the night I stayed up until three in the morning until he fell asleep so I could raise the blinds in the corner room like that cop asked me to.

They were in the house three seconds later. Dominic hadn't been kidding when he said they'd be patient. It's like they were two feet away from the front door all night long until Jarrod went to sleep. It was another one of those moments that felt more surreal than frightening. I have no idea how accurate my guess is, but with as loud as they were shouting and as fast as they moved, it was like there were two dozen men in SWAT uniforms. They came to the front door, the back door, the upstairs fire escape.

The girls started screaming, running around all over, but I was frozen in place.

Frozen in place when the men stormed Jarrod's room. I was right there with him. I remember looking for Dominic, but with the men in their full gear, how would I have known which was him?

Jarrod didn't fight back. They came in full protective gear with guns and assault rifles, but the cops didn't fire a single shot. Most likely, Jarrod knew how pointless it would be to resist. Maybe he put his confidence in his lawyers or in what he hoped was the state's inability to prove his guilt. For whatever reason, he didn't fight back, and the worst part was we'd actually had a really good evening together before that, just him and me.

Which is why I regretted helping the cops in the first place. Not that they needed me. I'm sure they could have gotten one of the other sister-wives to tell them where he slept or alert them when he went to bed, but now I would have to live with the knowledge that it was me.

Me, the one who'd been with Jarrod the longest. The one he still promised to buy a house for in Hawaii, just the two of us.

So Jarrod didn't resist when they came in, but I did. One of the SWAT men was acting too rough when he put the cuffs on. I could tell Jarrod was in pain, and I tried to push the cop away. He threw me back against the wall, and that's when another man called out, "Don't hurt her. She's the one who let us in." Maybe it was Dominic, maybe not. And like I said, all those helmets and things, impossible to know. But as soon as he said that, Jarrod looked at me with so much hurt and sadness in his eyes, which is why to this day I get a little choked up at the story of Jesus looking at Peter after he denies him those three times.

I'm sorry! I wanted to shout the words, but that would only prove my guilt even more. What had I been thinking? I should have warned Jarrod away, not led his attackers right to him. Struck with regret and remorse, I tried to prove my loyalty to my pimp the only way I knew how.

I attacked the two policemen closest to him, including the one who'd told his partner not to hurt me. Of course, when I was put on trial and charged with accessory to prostitution and the exploitation of minors, my behavior the night of Jarrod's arrest sealed my case against me.

I shouldn't complain, really. It could have been a lot worse. Prison was a much needed reprieve from my time in the stable and on the streets. True story. I was locked up with one of my sister-wives, and we grew even closer during that time. Not that I'd ever want to repeat those eighteen months, but as I look at my son and the way his father's got his hand on his shoulder, I realize I'm willing to serve time again if it means protecting Tyson. I can always count on my mom and dad to take my kid in if I get locked up. Always.

Jarrod leans down and tells my boy, "You stand right here. And don't even think of running, or I'll shoot your mom. Got it?"

Tyson nods obediently. I don't see any gun, but I know Jarrod well enough to know he's carrying.

Don't be stupid, boy, I want to tell my son. *Just give Mommy a few more minutes, and this will all be over.*

I hope.

Jarrod is right up against me now, his whole body trying to lean against mine. My inclination is to step away, but the more I back up, the farther I get from my kid. So I hold my breath, try not to show the disgust on my face, and wait for whatever's about to happen.

"I got a little proposal for you." Jarrod's voice is low, the same tone he used to sweet-talk me with so many years ago.

I will myself not to fall victim to his dizzying charm. I swear I'm a recovering addict, not just from the drugs and the alcohol but from him. How else can you explain how many times I went back to him, even after we both got out of jail?

"What do you want?" I'm disappointed that my voice quivers. I hope he doesn't think I'm afraid. He's like one of those wild animals. You can't let him sense your weakness.

"What do I want?" he repeats, so close his breath tickles my ear. "I'll give you one guess."

My whole body tenses when he kisses my neck. Every muscle wants to push him away, but he's dangerous and armed, and my kid is just a few feet away from us.

"Come on," I tell him. "Not here." I'm trying to calculate our survival chances if I grab Tyson's hand and run. How far would we get before Jarrod or one of his men gunned us down? Ten feet? Fifteen? I wonder if that old myth about running in a zigzag really makes you harder to shoot.

Maybe if it were only me I'd risk it, but I'm not about to put my son in that sort of danger. No matter what.

I squeeze my eyes shut and remind myself that whatever Jarrod wants to do to me, it's no worse than what's happened in the past. I'm not new to this game. And maybe if I keep my head on, if I don't freak out or shut down, I'll find a way to get me and my boy out of here safe.

His arm is around my waist. I seriously don't know what he expects to happen with my kid right here watching, but I'm not going to make any assumptions.

"Come on," I whisper, trying to sound compliant but firm at the same time. "Let's go somewhere else."

"But you haven't even heard my proposal."

I wonder how long I can stall him. But what would be the point? There's no help coming. It's just me and Tyson. Me and Tyson against Jarrod, his gun, and whoever he's hidden in the buildings around us. Or maybe I'm overreacting. Maybe he's alone. If I could figure out where he's got the weapon …

I let my arms slip around his waist.

"That's my girl."

I don't have to like what I'm doing. I just have to keep from barfing or gagging or turning into the kind of romantic puddle I used to whenever Jarrod got like this.

I remind myself of all the legal convictions against him. All his crimes against minors, including my own kid. Thank God Tyson doesn't look physically hurt, but how long's it going to take him to recover from the trauma of being stolen out of his bed in the middle of the night?

Jarrod is a monster. I repeat the words to myself, desperate to ward off the light-headedness I've started to feel at his touch. I told you I'm an addict, didn't I?

"You don't know how long I've waited to do this." His hands roam, and even when his touch turns painful I realize there's part of me that's missed him.

"You've gained weight," he says. He doesn't know about the pregnancy, at least I assume he doesn't, but the reminder that I have someone else's child in my womb snaps me out of whatever haze I've fallen into. Like the alcoholic who's about to jump off the wagon only to discover her drink's mixed with bleach.

I snatch these few moments of clarity, unable to guess when the mental fog might return. I run my hands up and down his back and chest, hoping that my frisking is taken for passionate enthusiasm. He leans in to kiss me, and that's when I feel the gun.

"Tyson, get down!" I shout and pull the weapon out of its holster. Problem is I've never shot a gun in my life. I squeeze the trigger but nothing happens except for Jarrod punching me in the jaw. I stumble to the ground, and the weapon flies out of my hand. Tyson's on his stomach, and I scurry to cover his body with my own, ready to sacrifice myself so the bullets don't reach him.

Jarrod's got the gun back. He's pointing it at us, so I crouch down even lower, praying to God that my body is thick enough to stop the bullets before they hit my son.

The crack of gunfire. My ears start to ring even before my mind registers the pain. I try to apologize to Tyson, tell him how much I love him, but I can't speak.

Another shot. I beg God to accept me into his kingdom in spite of all the terrible things I've done. Ask him to at least let my son grow up to live a long and happy life.

And then I wait, wondering if I'm going to feel myself die or if I'll just wake up blissfully in heaven.

CHAPTER 26

Something isn't right. I'm not dead. I don't even think I'm hurt. Is this one of those things where I'm shot but my adrenaline's rushing so hard I don't even know it? Does that really happen, or is that another one of those myths?

I hear shouting, but it's like I'm listening through water. Someone's leaning over me. At first I think it's Jarrod wondering if he's killed me yet, but I don't feel afraid.

Just cautiously curious. Like *what just happened to me?*

My son is stiff as a glass beer bottle beneath me. Did the bullet pass me and go straight into him? I don't know what's going on.

"It's ok. You can get up now." The hands that hold me are gentle, and before my brain can splice together all the different things happening, I'm being held against someone's chest, and he's stroking my hair telling me how much he loves me.

Except I know it's not Jarrod because my body's not reacting in fear. There's nothing about this embrace that feels dangerous. It's familiar. Like home.

"Damion?"

"Shhh," he whispers.

I know that there's nothing Jarrod would want more than to kill us both with one shot, so I try to pull him down to safety.

"You don't have to worry anymore." He nods toward the pavement, where my ex-boyfriend's body is lying in a puddle of blood. Detective Drisklay's scowling as he feels Jarrod's neck. Drisklay stands up, gives Jarrod a little kick with his shoe, and mumbles into his radio.

"He got him?" I ask.

Damion's burying his cheek against my hair. "Yeah, he got him."

"How'd he get here?"

Damion shrugs. "I called. Went over to the store across the street and used their phone."

It's so much to take in all at once. "Where's my baby?"

"He's here," Damion says, and I realize Tyson's between us. We're squeezing him so tight it's a miracle he can still breathe.

"You ok, baby?" I ask. He doesn't respond. I kneel down and face him, feeling him all over. "You hurt?"

He shakes his head.

"Poor kid's probably had the scare of his life," Damion says. I hold Tyson close and promise myself that starting right now, I'm going to stop being so impatient with my kid, so angry when he gets into problems in school. I'll be thankful for him every day, annoying and aggravating as he can be. So help me God.

Drisklay's holding his notebook in his hand. It's the first time I've seen him without a cup of coffee. "Want to tell me what happened?" he asks.

Damion clears his throat. Pulls me and Tyson close to him again. "Give us just a minute, detective. We're celebrating a Christmas miracle."

CHAPTER 27

The sun's nearly set by the time the three of us arrive back at Mom and Dad's, and we're all exhausted from those hours answering questions at the police station. Tyson finally perked up when he heard we were going to Grandma and Grandpa's for a late Christmas dinner. I hope he doesn't stay scared for too long.

Jarrod's good and dead. I guess Drisklay saw our little skirmish with the gun and shot him twice, once in the chest and once right in the skull. I tried not to let Tyson look, but he was curious. I think he might have seen the body. Just hope it doesn't give him too many nightmares.

Mom hasn't stopped hugging the three of us since we set foot in her house. I swear she's alternating between me and Tyson and Damion like we'd float away if we went longer than ten seconds without some sort of physical contact.

Dad's pretty overcome with emotion. He says a few harsh words about Jarrod and then apologizes right away. Tells my son that's no way to talk about anybody made in the image of God, no matter how evil their actions are. As for me, I'm still thinking about those old-fashioned Psalms, the ones about praying for God to smite your enemies and punish your foes. What is it that God says? *It is mine to avenge. I will repay.*

I don't know. I'm trying not to think about it too much right now. I'm so glad I have a son to focus all my energy and attention on. If it weren't for me knowing that Tyson's watching every move I make, I'd probably lose it. True story.

As it is, I manage to hold myself together while Dad prays for our Christmas dinner. He thanks God for protecting me and Tyson, thanks him for Damion's quick thinking and Detective

Drisklay's fast shot. He doesn't say anything about Jarrod, and I wonder if it does any good to pray for someone who's already dead. Not that I'd know how to pray for a monster like him.

Damion squeezes my hand when we're done. He had a lot of questions in the car on the ride here. Questions about Jesus and church and salvation. I told him to ask my dad and then I forgot about it, but I guess he was serious. First thing he says once dinner's served is if he can talk with my dad about Jesus after the meal.

Dad agrees of course, and he tells me I can come too if I want. Who knows, maybe I will.

Dinner's quiet. Not like last night with Mom and Dad and their forty guests. What do you say when your son's just been saved from his kidnapper who was shot in front of him?

Should I be glad Jarrod's dead? I don't know. I feel relief. Relief that my secret can remain my secret for however long I want it to. Relief that I never have to worry about going weak and crawling back to Jarrod like the addict I am.

Or was.

But am I glad he's dead? I'm not sure. I can still hear his voice in my head, telling me how much he loves me, how much he missed me when he was in prison. Then I look at Tyson, think about every horrible thing that could have happened to him.

Maybe I'll be glad in the morning. Right now, I'm just tired.

Tired and grateful to be alive.

CHAPTER 28

Dad and Damion shut themselves in the den right after dinner. Tyson's on the iPad trying to figure out what new game he's going to get with his gift certificate from his Christmas stocking. I'm helping Mom clean up, but she can tell something's wrong.

I swear one day I'll be sixty and she'll be ninety or something like that, and she'll still be able to tell when I'm keeping something from her.

"What is it, love?"

I shake my head. I don't want to talk about it, but I know I'm going to. That's just how Mom is. You can try to resist, but eventually she finds a way to draw all your woes and sorrows out. Sometimes it's healing and cathartic. Other times it's like trying to extract a tooth with nothing but a miniature ice pick.

"I'm just thinking." This is how I warm myself up. I still don't know what I'm going to tell her, so I say this to buy myself some time.

She sits down at the table and motions for me to join her. Once seated, I pick up my dirty fork and scrape some leftover green beans around on my plate.

"What's on your heart, pumpkin?"

I sigh, trying to summon the courage this is going to take. Maybe if I weren't pregnant, I wouldn't bother telling her. I'd keep it a secret like I have for so long. But the sonogram said it was a girl even though I've been convinced it's a boy, and part of me worries that until I get this off my chest, until I find forgiveness for this sin in my past, I'll somehow jinx my unborn child.

"You know you can tell me anything." Mom's holding my hand even though I don't remember her reaching for it. I glance in the living room to make sure Tyson isn't here. He can never learn what I'm about to say.

"It's just that seeing Jarrod again made me think about something that happened a long time ago," I begin. Mom doesn't reply. I stare past her shoulder so I don't have to make awkward eye contact, and I continue. "It started a few months before I moved in with you. Back when I was in junior high."

I steal a quick glance. Mom's face is serious. I can't watch. Can't look at her expression when I confess what I did to that little baby girl so many years ago.

My voice is flat and expressionless. I tell her everything, down to the most intricate detail. The little fuzz on the skin. The way my baby hardly cried at all. The only thing I don't mention is how she stared into my eyes.

I can't stand to let Mom see me. I cover my face, but she leans in and lets me hide against her shoulder. Ten seconds later her shirt sleeve is drenched with my tears.

"I killed her," I sob. "I didn't know what to do, and I was all alone, and I left her there to die."

Mom strokes my hair. It's almost painful, her touch is so gentle and loving. I deserve a beating. Another prison sentence. Anything but this.

I shake my head. "I killed my little girl." I keep waiting for Mom to state the obvious. That there's no way to know for sure if she died. That she could have been rescued. Maybe someone found her that night. Maybe she was adopted into a loving home, far more stable than what I could ever have hoped to offer.

But all she says is, "How long ago was this exactly?"

I tell her.

She's looking at some pictures on the fridge. Gets up and goes over to pull down one of those fancy senior photos teens get before they graduate. She hands it to me.

"Who's this?" I ask.

Mom sits. Rubs my back slowly and carefully, like she's afraid I might break if she goes too fast or presses too hard.

"That's one of the foster daughters who came to live with us. You remember Tiffany?"

"Yeah, she graduated pretty recently, didn't she?" I squint. I never took the time to get to know any of Mom and Dad's most recent foster kids, but I do remember seeing this one around even though I didn't bother to keep track of her name.

Mom sighs. "A few years ago, we told the state we were interested in adopting her."

"Oh." I don't know what else to say. What in the world does this have to do with me?

"There was a problem with the paperwork though," Mom continues. "Couldn't figure out how to get in touch with her birth mother."

"Yeah?"

She nods. "See, a while back, a baby was born and put into the foster system. By the time she came to live with us, there was some sort of mix-up with her file. When our case worker approached the birth mom to talk about signing off parental rights, the woman was confused. Yes, she had a child in the system, but it wasn't Tiffany, this little girl who'd been born in a middle school bathroom."

Mom pauses to let the words sink in, but I'm afraid my brain's shutting down. I can't think, can't process, can't feel.

"We told them we still wanted to adopt her, but they said they'd have to try to track down the real birth mom. Didn't apologize for their mistake, didn't tell us how long it would take. By the time Tiffany graduated and moved out west, it was too late. Far as I know, the state still can't figure out who delivered Tiffany Franklin."

"Her last name's Franklin?"

Mom shrugs. "Don't ask me where it came from. We may never know what happened between the time someone found her and the state made such a mess out of her file. But I do know one thing. That daughter you've been mourning over, the one you've felt so guilty over for so long, is a high-school graduate, a beautiful young woman, and she's living out on her own in Washington and doing just fine."

CHAPTER 29

I've been sitting in the guest room for an hour or more. Sitting here and staring at this picture. My mind refuses to accept that this young woman could be the same little baby who'd held my gaze two decades ago. She's all grown up now. How could that have happened?

I'm sorry, I whisper to the girl in the photo. Tiffany. Tiffany Franklin.

I'm sorry, I repeat. Mom tells me I shouldn't feel guilty. After all, Jarrod had wanted me to get rid of her. If he had been with me the day she was delivered, she would have never survived. Mom says I should feel proud that I gave my child life.

I suppose that's one way to look at it. The other way to look at it was that I was so afraid of losing Jarrod, so dependent on him, so in love that it was easier for me to abandon a perfect little baby in a filthy trash can than to find someone to ask for help.

Forgiveness comes so easily to Mom. It's harder for me.

She told me a little bit about Tiffany. About how she gave her life to Jesus at a church youth group event, about how well she did in high school, how bright she is. I realize that those afternoons when Mom would babysit my son, Tyson was in the same house as his biological sister.

I can't even.

Mom told me that if I wanted her to, she could introduce me to this woman who through some twisted work of fate or divine intervention is both my daughter and my foster sibling.

"I don't know if I'm ready for that yet," I told her. Thankfully, Mom seemed to understand. She didn't get all pushy.

Should I take Mom up on her offer? Should I let this young woman know who I am? I still can't believe I was coming over to this house two or three times a week to drop my son off or pick him up and my daughter was here.

That whole time and none of us suspected a thing?

I'm startled by the sound of the door. Damion clears his throat and comes in. "Am I interrupting anything?"

I slip the photo between the pages of the Bible on the nightstand. "No, I'm just resting."

He sits down on the bed beside me.

"Did you have a good talk with my dad?" I ask before he can question me about the photo I've hidden.

He nods. There's something in his eyes. An almost radiance. "It was really neat. I wish you would have been there."

I shrugged. "Yeah, well, I've heard it all by now, I'm sure."

"But that's the thing." Damion's speaking twice as fast as normal. Does he have any idea how tired I am? Any idea what sort of heaviness is hanging over my spirit after all that's happened today? "I thought I'd heard it all too, but your dad has this way of helping things make so much more sense."

I glance over just to make sure that this really is my boyfriend and not some stranger. "What kinds of things did you talk about?"

"How to know if God's really forgiven you, how to know for sure if you'll go to heaven. How it's not about how good we are but if we've trusted Jesus to forgive us. And a whole bunch of other things. We were in there for a really long time."

I glance at the clock. "Were you?"

He scoots closer to me and takes my hand in his. "One of the other things we talked about is how big a step marriage really is."

Now I'm giving him my attention. Is he changing his mind about the engagement? Did my dad convince him to break up with me?

"I know we haven't done things perfect, but I want that to change," he explains.

Yup. He's breaking up with me. I can't even.

Thanks, Dad. Perfect timing, and merry Christmas to you too.

"What kind of changes?" I ask cautiously.

"We can talk about all that after."

"After what?"

That's when he slides off the bed and gets down on his knee, still holding my hand. "After I give you this ring back. That is, if you'll take it."

In spite of everything — today's trauma, my exhaustion, the fact that I have an adult daughter Damion doesn't even know about — I smile. "Are you asking me to?"

He's grinning too. "Better believe it. Can I put it on?"

"Yes."

"Yes?" he repeats. "You really mean it? Your answer's yes?"

"Yes." I chuckle. How many times do I have to say it?

He slips the ring on my finger and beams. "Perfect fit."

I don't tell him the truth, that until I get over the rest of this pregnancy and stop being so bloated, the ring is way too tight. But after this daughter — or son — of ours is born, it will work just fine.

"Perfect fit," I agree, and he hugs me.

"Merry Christmas," he says and kisses the top of my head.

I pull him to his feet and kiss him lightly on the lips. Tipping my chin back, I gaze up into his face and smile. "Merry Christmas."

FROM THE AUTHOR

Ready for even more heart-stopping suspense? Are you searching for a Christian fiction series that shows life like it is, doesn't pull any punches, and raises tough questions about hot-button issues without holding your hand and telling you what to believe?

If you think Blessing went through a lot, meet Kennedy Stern, a missionary kid who's about to find out that surviving college is harder than she ever imagined.

(Literally.)

Kennedy's childhood on the mission field did nothing to prepare her for the intense homesickness, grueling academic schedule, or moral dilemmas she'd face at Harvard.

Of course, she wasn't planning to encounter kidnappers, stalkers, and terrorists either. Kennedy's college career reads like one big thriller series, exciting as any Hollywood blockbuster, and packed full of controversy, danger, and dilemmas.

These edge-of-your-seat novels are guaranteed to keep you thinking (and guessing) at all hours of the night. Start the award-winning Kennedy Stern Christian suspense series today ... Just be prepared to stay up late!

Read *Unplanned* by Alana Terry today.

Made in United States
Orlando, FL
11 February 2025